Stories for 3 Year Olds

Stories for Year Olds

3

LITTLE TIGER PRESS

London

Contents

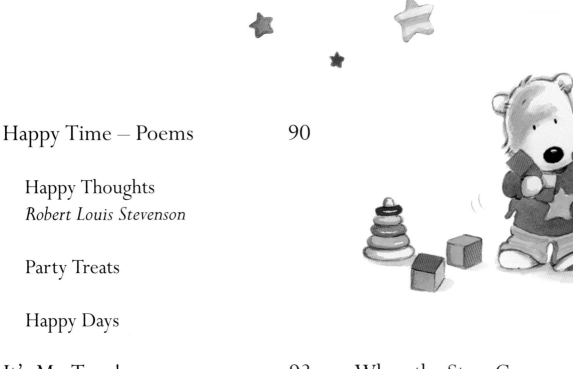

Little Bear's Big Jumper

David Bedford   Caroline Pedler

Big Bear loved his stripy jumper.
It was warm. It was soft. And it
was his very favourite.

   But it was getting harder and
harder to put on.

   "It's too small for you!" said
Little Bear, giggling.

   "It's not," said Big Bear.
"It fits just right!"

Mum laughed. "I think
it's time I knitted you
a new jumper, Big Bear.
Why don't you give that
one to your brother?"

"But it's too big
for him," said
Big Bear.
   "No it's not,"
said Little Bear.

He pulled it quickly
over his head.
   "It fits just right!"

"You'd better look after it,"
said Big Bear. "It's my
favourite jumper — EVER."
"I will," said Little Bear,
happily. "It's my favourite
ever too!"

Off they ran together
to play. "Now I look just
like you!" cried Little Bear.

Big Bear gave his brother a piggyback
through the tall grass. Little Bear
chuckled as he was jiggled about.

The two brothers jumped through
the puddles with a
Splish! Splash! Splosh!
"This is fun!" said Big Bear.

Then Big Bear
climbed along a
high branch.
"I'm climbing too!"
said Little Bear.
"You're pulling
me down,"
cried his brother.
"Get off!"

"I can wibble-wobble like you!" said Little Bear.
"Stop it!" said Big Bear. "You're wobbling
too much!"
And suddenly . . .

. . . Crack! went the log,
as it split in two.
Sploosh!
went the bears as they landed
in a muddy puddle.

"Look what you've done!" yelled Big Bear. "You've broken the wobbly log. And you've made a mess of MY jumper!"

Little Bear looked down at
the soggy jumper. His lip
began to tremble.

"I'm s-o-r-r-y!" he said,
and he ran away into the
woods.

"Good then," said Big Bear,
grumpily. "It's better playing
on my own."

Big Bear slid down the slippery-slidey
slope. He chased a butterfly until
he was dizzy. Then he sat on
the end of the see-saw.
But with only one
bear, it wouldn't
go up or down.

*Playing is no fun
without Little Bear,*
he thought. And he
began to feel very lonely.
"Where ARE you,
Little Bear?"

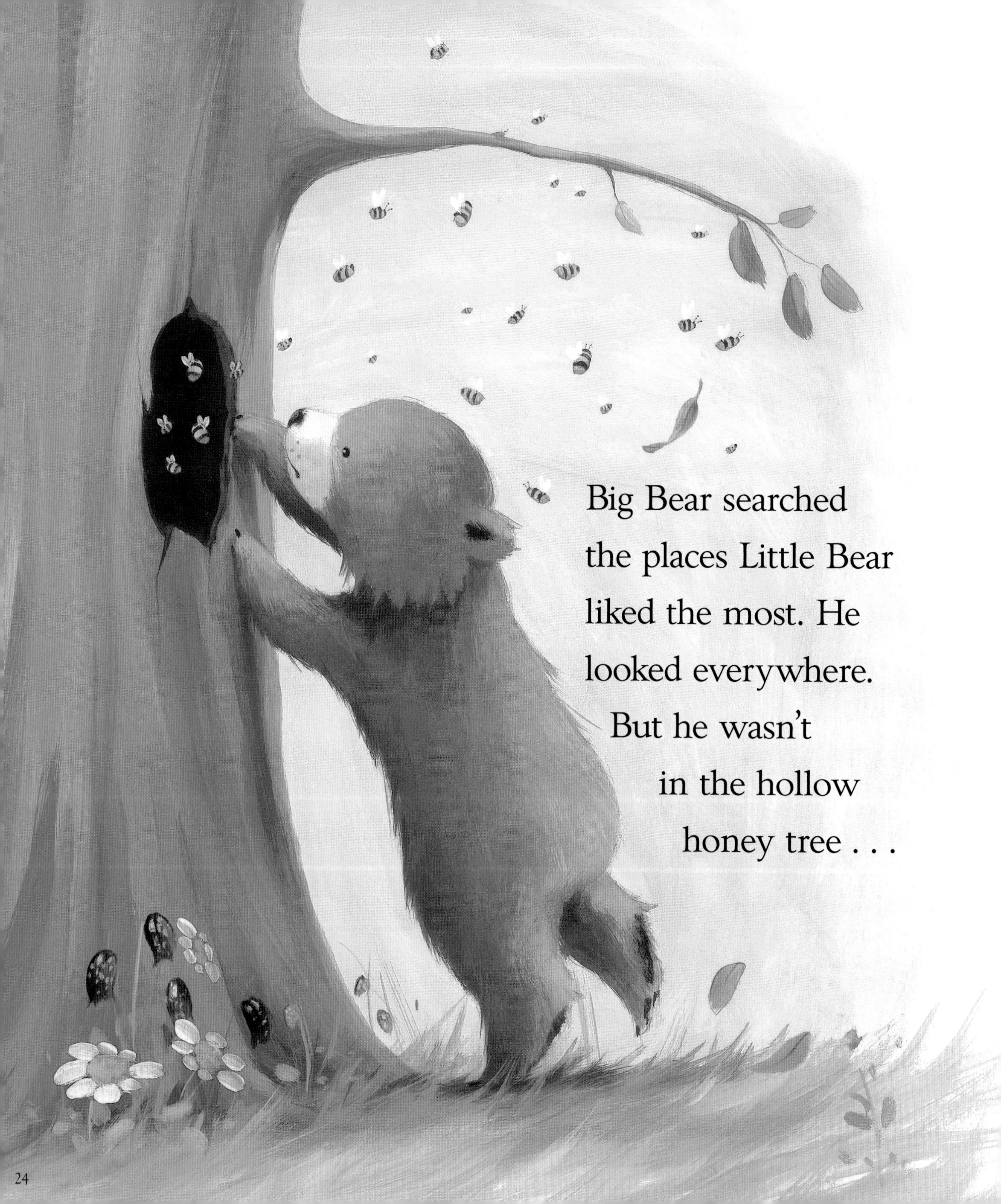

Big Bear searched
the places Little Bear
liked the most. He
looked everywhere.
But he wasn't
in the hollow
honey tree . . .

or in their den
in the bush . . .

He wasn't even hiding under
the big rock.

Little Bear wasn't anywhere!

Where could he have

got to, all on

his own?

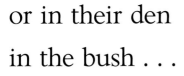

Suddenly, Big Bear saw a woolly thread. So he followed it quickly through the trees, round a bush and deeper and deeper into the woods, until at last he found . . .

. . . a very sad and
lonely Little Bear.

"I've ruined our favourite ever jumper!" Little Bear cried when he saw him.

Big Bear gave his brother a big hug.
"Don't worry," he said, kindly.
"It's only a jumper! I'm sorry
I shouted at you."

"It's all right,"
Little Bear
sniffed. "I
shouldn't have
run off."

Big Bear
took him by
the hand.
"Let's go home,"
he said.

On the way back,
Big Bear wrapped
up all the wool
into a ball.

"We had a little accident,"
he told Mum when they
got home.
"Poor Little Bear!"
said Mum. "Don't worry,
I know just what to do."

The very next morning,
Big Bear and Little Bear
had the best surprise . . .
two brand new, matching,
stripy jumpers!

"Now I can be just like
you, Little Bear!" said
Big Bear. "You're the best
brother EVER!"

Fun in the Sun

From a Railway Carriage

Faster than fairies, faster than witches,

Bridges and houses, hedges and ditches;

And charging along like troops in a battle

All through the meadows the horses and cattle:

All of the sights of the hill and the plain

Fly as thick as driving rain;

And ever again, in the wink of an eye,

Painted stations whistle by.

~ Robert Louis Stevenson

Long Beach Days

Pat a sandcastle,
Find a seashell.
Stick in a flag,
And some seaweed as well.

Quick! Grab the bucket
Race to the sea
Up to my knees now,
Yay – look at me!

Sunny Day

Hip-hooray,
A sunny day!
Skip outside –
It's time to play!

Pirate
Piggy Wiggy

Diane and Christyan Fox

Sometimes when I sail my little boats, I dream of what it might be like to be a swashbuckling pirate!

I would wear
a big black hat,
a patch over my eye
and have a parrot
on my shoulder . . .

My ship would be
the finest that
ever sailed
the seven
seas.

On hot, sunny days we could walk the plank!

At night-time we
could sit around
the fire singing
sea shanties. . .

On Crossbone Island we would search for treasure.

Ten paces north . . .
eight paces south . . .

Shiver-me-timbers, X marks the spot!

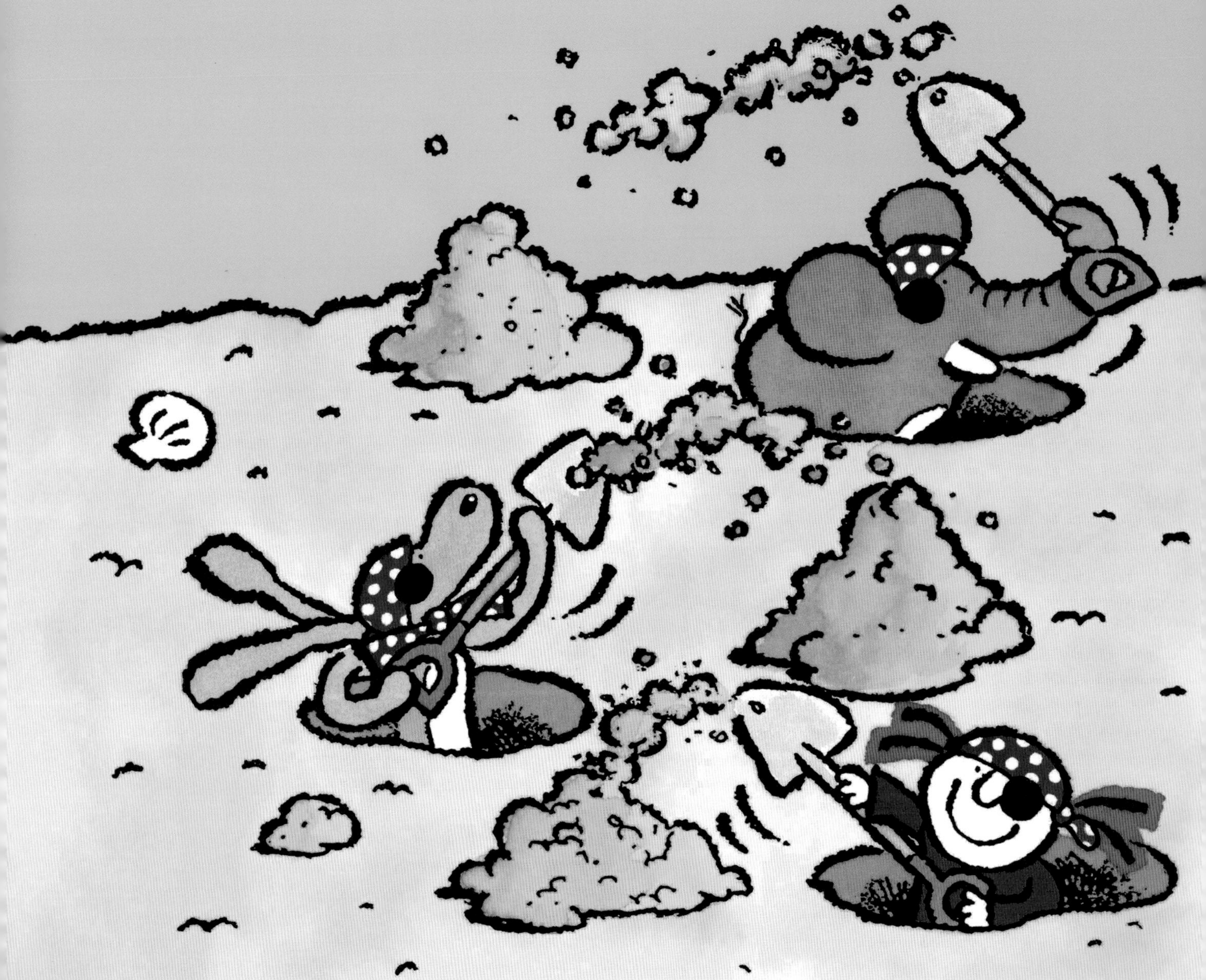

The richest treasure
ever seen . . .

But we'd have to sail back home again

to find the treasure
we love best!

In the Garden

Caterpillar

Brown and furry
Caterpillar in a hurry,
Take your walk
To the shady leaf, or stalk,
Or what not,
Which may be the chosen spot.

~ Christina Rossetti

Have You Watched the Fairies?

Have you watched the fairies
when the rain is done
Spreading out their little wings
to dry them in the sun?
I have, I have! Isn't it fun?

~ Rose Fyleman

The Ladybird

Some lucky ladybirds have six big black spots,
And some little ones just have four.
Sometimes I count spots –
one two three STOP! STOP!
See it fly off before I can count any more!

Butterfly

Butterflies dance in butterfly sky.
Butterflies swoop and spin when they fly.
Butterflies drift and butterflies roam.
Flutter on, butterflies – all the way home!

The Busy Busy Day

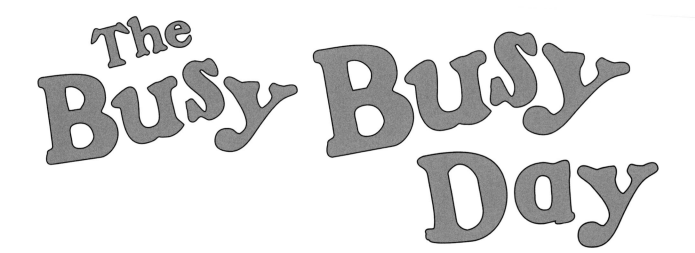

Claire Freedman   Daniel Howarth

"Hooray! Spring is here!" cried Ginger, tugging on his old boots. "Come on, Floppy, let's go and do some gardening."

They marched outside and looked around.

"What shall we do first, Ginger?" asked Floppy excitedly.

"I know!" said Ginger. "Let's clear away those logs."
And he went to get the wheelbarrow.

CHIRP!   CHIRP!   CHIRP!

Two worried-looking robins swooped down.

"Hmmm, something's bothering them," said
Ginger. "I can't see anything wrong, can you?"

"No!" said Floppy, shaking his head. "Perhaps
they think we want to eat their worms!"

They looked in the wheelbarrow and couldn't believe their eyes. Snug in one corner lay a nestful of baby robins!

CHEEP! CHEEP! CHEEP!

"So that's why the robins were chirping," said Ginger. "They thought we might frighten their baby chicks. We mustn't disturb them."

"What shall we do now, Ginger?" Floppy asked.

"Hmm," said Ginger thoughtfully. "Well, we can't clear away the logs without a wheelbarrow. We'll do another job instead."

They started to pick up the flowerpots and stack them.

Oh! Now Ginger had found something else. "Come and look at this, Floppy," he whispered. "But be very, very quiet!"

Inside the biggest flowerpot, two tiny hedgehogs were curled up, fast asleep. They snuffled and snored noisily.

"Oooh!" gasped Floppy excitedly. "Don't they look funny!"

"Shhh, don't say a word!" Ginger hushed. "We mustn't wake them!"

They both tiptoed away without a sound.

"Well, Floppy," said Ginger. "We can't sort out the flowerpots. But we can tidy up the shed." And he opened the shed door.

EEEK! EEEK! EEEK!

"That's not the door creaking," said Ginger. "Is it you making that funny noise, Floppy?"

"No!" Floppy giggled. "Maybe your old boots are squeaking, Ginger."

"It's not me *or* my boots," Ginger replied. "So what can it be?"

Floppy peered along the dusty shelves
between the boxes and baskets.

"Atchoo!" he sneezed.

Ginger checked the bulb packets. Floppy
tipped the watering can upside down.

Nothing!

EEEK! EEEK!

"There it goes again, Floppy!" said Ginger.
"What is it?"

"I don't know," said Floppy. "But it's a
very loud squeak!"

Ginger sat down by some seed trays to think
what it could be . . . and very nearly squashed
a family of mice!

"Goodness, that was close!" said Ginger.
"So *that's* what was squeaking! Well, we can't
tidy up the shed now. We might disturb
the mice!"

Ginger closed the shed door quietly behind them. "Don't worry, Floppy!" he said. "We can still do the weeding."

Floppy kneeled beside the flowerbeds.
A big orange butterfly landed on his nose.

"Hee hee!" laughed Floppy. "That tickles!"

"Aha!" Ginger said to Floppy.
"I think the butterflies are trying to tell us something!"

"What could *that* be?"
said Floppy in surprise.

Ginger looked closely at the dandelion leaves.

"Just as I thought," he said. "Caterpillars!
One day they'll grow into butterflies
too. No more weeding
till then!"

Ginger and Floppy walked back up the garden,
and Ginger pulled off his old boots.

"Our garden may not be tidy," he said,
looking around, "but I think it's perfect just
the way it is!"

"You're right, Ginger," Floppy
agreed happily. "It's
perfect for all our
little friends
and . . ."

". . . it's just perfect for a sunny picnic too!"

Ginger fetched the picnic blanket. Floppy brought out some orangeade and cakes.

"Everyone can enjoy our garden," Ginger said cheerfully as he tucked in.

And everyone did!

Happy Time

Happy Thoughts

The world is so full of a number of things,
I'm sure we should all be as happy as kings.

~ Robert Louis Stevenson

Party Treats

Jelly in my tum-tum,
Squishy cake galore.
Sweet and gooey fun-fun –
Can I have some more?

Happy Days

On rainy days, I play outside.
I splash in puddles – slip and slide!

On sunny days, I'm in the sea,
With water splashing at my knee.

On windy days, I race and swoop.
Just like a plane – I loop-the-loop!

On snowy days, I wear my hat,
And scoop up snowballs – squish, squash, SPLAT!

Oh, what a lot of games I've found,
In every weather, all year round!

It's My Turn!

David Bedford   Elaine Field

Oscar and Tilly found a playground.
"Shall we play on the slide?" asked Oscar.
"I'll go first," said Tilly.

"I'll go now," said Oscar.
"Not yet," said Tilly.
"It's not your turn."

"That looks fun,"
said Oscar.
"Is it my turn now?"
"Not yet," said Tilly.

Tilly went round and round on the roundabout.

"Is it my turn yet?" asked Oscar.

"No," said Tilly. "I haven't finished."

Tilly went round

 and round

  and round

   and ROUND . . . .

"I feel dizzy,"
said Tilly.

"Hee, hee," cried Oscar.
"It's my turn now,
you're too wobbly!"

"This is fun."

"I feel better now," said Tilly.
"Can I slide after you?"
"No," said Oscar. "It's not your turn."

"Can I go on the swing after you?"
asked Tilly.
"No," said Oscar. "It's still my turn."

"Get off, Tilly," shouted Oscar.

"It's my turn on the see-saw."

"The see-saw doesn't work," said Tilly.

But when Oscar jumped on the other end . . .

... Tilly went up in the air!

Then Tilly
came down
and . . .

113

Oscar went up . . .

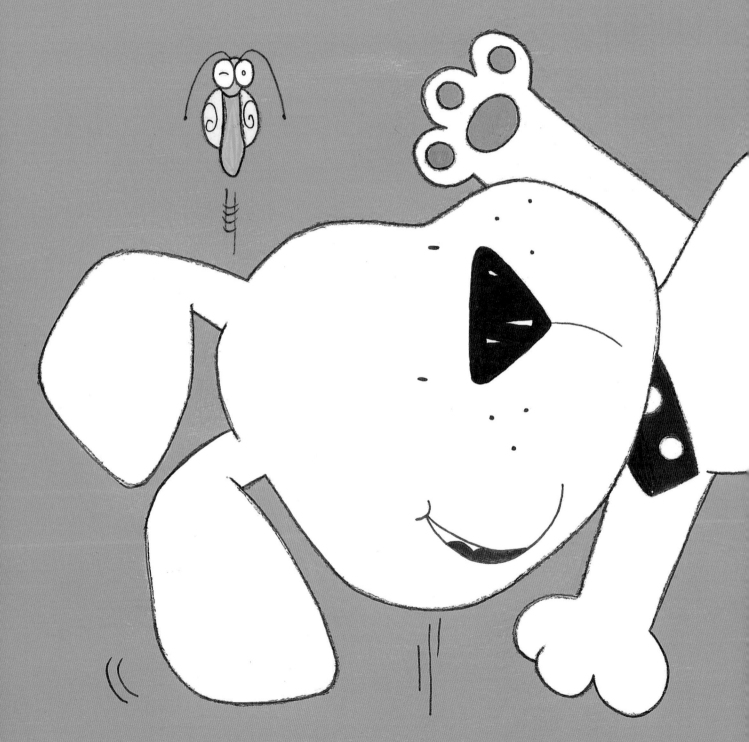

WHOO

and then . . .

WHOO

Oscar and Tilly
played together
all afternoon.

Silly Time

If a Pig Wore a Wig

If a pig wore a wig,
What could we say?
Treat him as a gentleman,
And say "Good day."

~ Christina Rossetti

The Snake and the Mittens

I fear I made a dreadful mistake,
When I knitted mittens for a snake.
He said, "'Twas kind of you to knit,
But I just don't think they'll ever fit."

Anna Elise

Anna Elise, she jumped with surprise;

The surprise was so quick, it played her a trick;

The trick was so rare, she jumped in a chair;

The chair was so frail, she jumped in a pail;

The pail was so wet, she jumped in a net;

The net was so small, she jumped on the ball;

The ball was so round, she jumped on the ground;

And ever since then she's been turning around.

A Friend Like You

Julia Hubery

Caroline Pedler

Panda stretched happily in the morning sun. It was the first day of spring, time for his special journey up into the mountains.

Sunlight sparkled in the trees as Panda walked through the peaceful forest. Suddenly, a nut hit him on the nose. It was Monkey!

"Where are you going, Panda?" he giggled. "Anywhere fun?"

"Somewhere with a beautiful
secret," said Panda. "Do you want
to come too?"

"Yes please!" squealed Monkey.
"I love secrets!"

As they set off, Monkey danced around
Panda, hurrying him along. "Come on,"
he squeaked. "I want to see the secret!"

"Slow down, little friend," said Panda. "It's
a long way. We have to cross Silver River
first, then follow the rocky stream to the
mountain meadows."

"That sounds easy," said Monkey. "Let's
get going, Panda-plod!" And he raced ahead.

Panda padded on in the leafy
shade. As he stopped to chew
some bamboo, he heard a
chirrup under the leaves.
There he found a lovely bird,
bright as a jewel.

"Monkey, come and see this!" he called.

But Monkey was out of sight.

"Poor Monkey," thought Panda.

"In such a rush, he never sees anything!

I wonder where he's got to?"

Before long, Panda
found him chasing
his tail round a tree.
"You've been ages," said Monkey,
"and I couldn't find the silly river!"
"If you hush a minute, you'll hear it,"
said Panda. "We're almost there."

"But I'm too excited to hush!" laughed Monkey, chattering away as they strolled on together.

Soon they reached
the banks of Silver River.
"I'm going to swing across,"
boasted Monkey. "Watch me fly, Panda!"
"Be careful!" Panda called out, as Monkey
leaped up into the branches.
Panda swam slowly down into the cool
water, smiling as a shoal of flickering fish
tickled by his toes.

Monkey came swinging
through the treetops.
  "I'll beat you across,
old soggy-ploddy-bear!"
he shouted.

One,

two,

three,

Whheeeeee

look at

Meeeeee!

Monkey let go of his branch,
and soared up, up through
the glorious sky . . .

. . . then down,

Splash!

into the river.

"Help!" he shrieked.

"Here I am," shouted Panda. "Hold on tight!"
He pulled the squidgy, shivering monkey
from the water and swam to the shore.

"Poor little Monkey-mess! However did
I find a friend like you?" Panda laughed.
"Come on — have a ride on my back!"
Monkey snuggled into Panda's cosy fur.
"Thank you, Panda," he whispered.

Up and up Panda climbed through the misty foothills.

"Monkey, did you ever see anything so pretty?" he gasped, but there was no answer. Monkey was fast asleep.

"Sleep well, little friend," Panda whispered, and padded softly on.

At last they reached the lush green meadows.
"Are we there?" squeaked Monkey,
bouncing awake. "Can I see the secret now?"
"It's up in the highest meadow," said Panda.
"The mountain butterflies are about to fly —
it's an amazing sight!"

"Quick, I want to see them!" Monkey squealed.

"Wait!" called Panda. "I can't keep up."

"But they'll fly away!" Monkey cried,
skipping off. Panda sighed sadly and
climbed slowly after him.

When Panda reached the top, Monkey was looking very cross. "There aren't any butterflies!" he snapped. "We've missed them, all because you're such a slowcoach!"

"That's not very fair," cried Panda. "I can't rush like you. It's just the way I am."

Monkey hung his head. "I'm sorry, Panda," he said.
"I know I'm lucky to have a friend like you."

Panda smiled. "Don't worry, little Monkey,"
he said gently. "All we have to do now is
wait — ever so quiet, and ever so still."

Monkey snuggled next to Panda, and
slowly, slowly, slowly . . .

. . . a thousand butterflies stretched their wings,
and flew into the air.

"They're amazing!" Monkey whispered.
"Thank you, Panda."

Panda hugged him and smiled. "I'm happy
I can share them with a friend like you."

When the Stars Come Out

Stars on High

One, two – stars on high,

Three, four – in the sky,

Five, six – burning bright,

Seven, eight – in the night,

Nine, ten – I declare,

Too many stars to count up there!

Goodnight!

Goodnight! Goodnight!
Far flies the light.
But still God's love,
Shall flame above,
Making all bright.
Goodnight!

~ Victor Hugo

Night

The sun descending in the west
The evening star does shine,
The birds are silent in their nest
And I must seek for mine.

~ William Blake

By the Light of the Silvery Moon

Claire Freedman

Steve Gulbis

Down on the farm,
the moon is up,
And night-time
is starting to fall.
But Little Grey Hare
is wide awake,
He's not feeling
sleepy at all.

"Look at the moon!"
cries Little Grey Hare.
"Mummy, it's shining
so bright!
"Let's play!" he calls to the
woolly white lambs,
And they scamper off
into the night.

White moonbeams dance
on the henhouse roof.
The chicks should be
curled up asleep.
But out they all tumble,
one by one.
"Let's go and explore,"
they cheep.

Tucked in their sty,
the piglets can't sleep.
"Let's play a game!"
they say.
A shooting star
streaks past the moon,
As they romp in the
sweet, fresh hay.

Little Hare hops
to the moonlit pond.
The ducklings
are splashing about.
"Back to the nest,"
Mummy Duck quacks.
"But we want to play
games!" they shout.

"It's sleepy-time now!"
Mummy Cat calls.
She searches each
hiding place.
"But we're not ready!"
the kittens miaow,
And out of the farmyard
they race.

It's very late now,
and everyone's tired.
It's bedtime for
small sleepyheads!
So yawning and sighing,
away they all creep,
Back home to their
cosy, warm beds.

Last one asleep
is Little Grey Hare,
So snug on the soft,
mossy floor.
"Hush!" sighs his mummy,
"Sleep tight," smiles the moon,
And the only sound now
is a snore!

STORIES FOR 3 YEAR OLDS

LITTLE TIGER PRESS
1 The Coda Centre
189 Munster Road
London SW6 6AW
www.littletiger.co.uk

First published in Great Britain 2013

Printed in China

LTP/1800/0932/0514

ISBN 978-1-84895-730-5

4 6 8 10 9 7 5 3

LITTLE BEAR'S BIG JUMPER

David Bedford
Illustrated by Caroline Pedler

First published in Great Britain 2008
by Little Tiger Press

PIRATE PIGGY WIGGY

Diane and Christyan Fox

First published in Great Britain 2003
by Little Tiger Press

THE BUSY BUSY DAY

Claire Freedman
Illustrated by Daniel Howarth

First published in Great Britain 2004
by Little Tiger Press

ACKNOWLEDGEMENTS

'Stars on High' by Stephanie Stansbie, copyright © Little Tiger Press 2008;
'Long Beach Days', 'Butterfly', 'Party Treats', 'Happy Days' by Stephanie Stansbie,
copyright © Little Tiger Press 2013;
'Sunny Day', 'The Ladybird', 'The Snake and the Mittens' by Mara Alperin,
copyright © Little Tiger Press 2013

Additional artwork by Rachel Baines, copyright © Little Tiger Press 2010, 2013

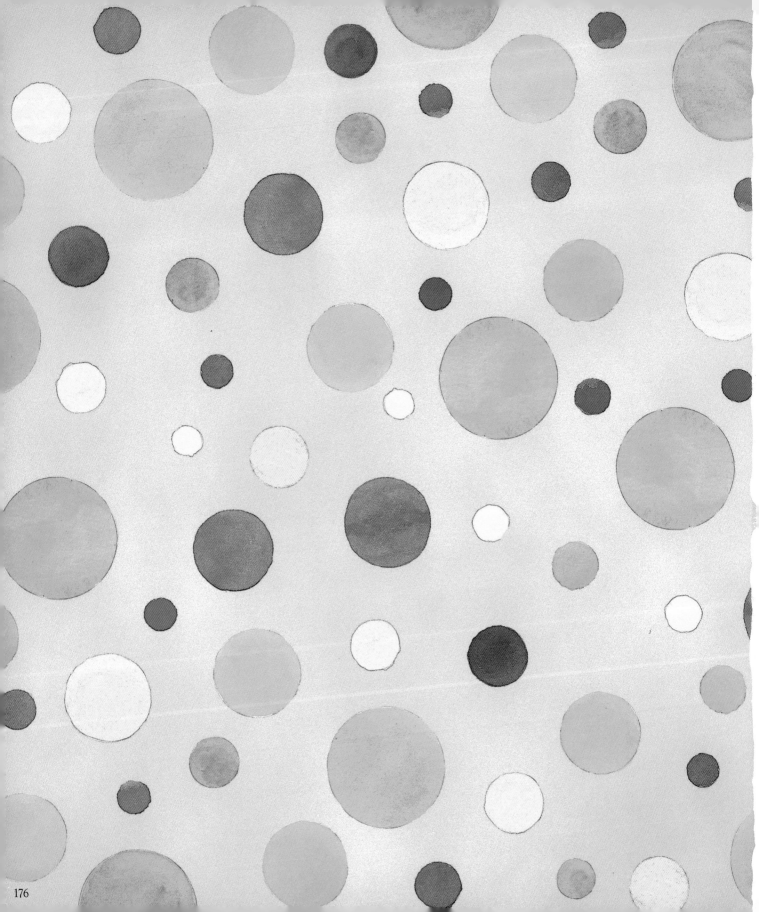

THE
NATION'S
FAVOURITE
FOOD FAST

THE NATION'S FAVOURITE FOOD

FAST!
NEVEN MAGUIRE

100
BEST-LOVED
RECIPES FOR
BUSY LIVES

GILL & MACMILLAN

Gill & Macmillan
Hume Avenue
Park West
Dublin 12
www.gillmacmillanbooks.ie

© Neven Maguire 2014
www.nevenmaguire.com
978 07171 6220 8

Compiled by Orla Broderick
Edited by Kristin Jensen
Designed by www.grahamthew.com
Photography © Joanne Murphy
Food styling by Sharon Hearne-Smith
Kitchen assistants: Joanna Carley, Olivia Raftery, Stacey Carr,
Paul McHugh, Claire Beasley and Sarah Watchorn
Indexed by Eileen O' Neill
Printed by L.E.G.O. SpA

Props
31 Chapel Lane (a merchant for Irish linen and tweed),
Tullyvin, Co. Cavan: www.31chapellane.com
Avoca, Kilmacanogue Store, Café & HQ, Wicklow: www.avoca.ie
Article Dublin, Powerscourt Townhouse, South William St, Dublin:
(01) 679 9268; www.articledublin.com
Meadows and Byrne, The Pavilion, Royal Marine Road, Dún
Laoghaire, Co. Dublin: (01) 280 4554; www.meadowsandbyrne.com
Two Wooden Horses, Chapel Road, Greystones, Co. Wicklow:
www.twowoodenhorses.com

This book is typeset in 11pt Brandon Grotesque on 14pt.

The paper used in this book comes from the wood pulp of managed
forests. For every tree felled, at least one tree is planted, thereby
renewing natural resources.

A CIP catalogue record for this book is available from the
British Library.

This book is dedicated to Eileen,
my wonderful mother-in-law, who is a
whizz kid in the kitchen. Thank you for
all your love and kindness to me and
the twins. You're a star!

ACKNOWLEDGEMENTS

This book simply could not have happened without my long-term collaborator and dear friend, Orla Broderick. It's a pleasure to work with you.

Thanks to Olivia Rafferty, who has been a huge help to me in setting up my dream – my very own cookery school!

Sharon Hearne-Smith is a talented food stylist and, apart from this book, she also works on my television shows. I am always thrilled with the results. Thanks also to Claire Beasley, Paul McHugh, Stacey Corr, Joanna Carley and Sharon Watchorn for all their work testing the recipes – I know they enjoyed eating the results!

A special thank you to my hard-working and very loyal head chef Glen Wheeler and sous chef Carmel McGirr, who organised all of the food for the photography and recipe testing. Your help is very much appreciated.

Thanks to Joanne Murphy for her stunning photography and Graham Thew for his fresh design – another triumph! What a talent. The 'A-Team' at Gill & Macmillan were a pleasure to work with as usual. A special thanks to Nicki Howard for her amazing vision, dedication and passion – I have huge admiration and respect for you and your work. Thanks to Catherine Gough, Kristin Jensen and Teresa Daly for all their work, and thank you to Michael Gill for his personal interest. You did it again!

RTÉ has played a huge part in my career. It began when John Masterson, my agent, believed in me and gave me my first break on *Open House* in 1998 – I can't thank him enough for that and for his friendship and support. Thank you to Brian Walsh for his continued support – I admire his passion for food. To David Hare, who produces my TV shows, thank you for always showing my best side – you are a true gent to work with. Thanks also to Billy Keady and Ray de Brún.

Thank you to Purcell Masterson for advice and support over the years and thanks particularly to Mary Tallent, Brigid O'Dea and the whole Purcell Masterson team. Thanks also to Colm Bradley from Hype & Holler for all your innovative ideas and great work on social media.

A big thank you to Bord Bia for their continued support, especially Aidan Cotter and Theresa Brophy. A huge thank you also to Hylda Adams, who has been a great mentor to me throughout my career. I can't thank you enough.

Thank you to all the media of which there are too many to mention – the list would go on and on! Thank you so much for all of your support and loyalty throughout my career.

Thank you to Eoin O'Flynn at Flogas for his continued support and friendship, and to Kenneth Maguire, my brother, and Andrea Doherty for organising all my demos and making sure things run smoothly.

To my team at the restaurant, who I consider part of the family, a big thanks for all of your hard work and loyalty. You are what makes the MacNean Restaurant a success. A particular thanks to Kevin Ashley, whose love and passion for growing all of our salads, herbs and vegetables is infectious.

Thank you to all my supporters and the people I meet all over the country. You provide such inspiration and give me great feedback about my recipes. I hope you will enjoy this book as much as my last. Have fun and enjoy the recipes!

Finally, I feel very lucky and privileged to have come from a very close family. Thank you for all your love and support. I hope you enjoy this book.

Neven

CONTENTS

INTRODUCTION

I've been overwhelmed by your reaction to my last book, *The Nation's Favourite Food*. People have come up to me and said they call it their 'kitchen bible', or have sent in letters thanking me for inspiring them to create delicious dishes. One lady told me she responds to the compliments her cooking receives with 'Me and Neven Maguire'!

I feel like I was put on this earth to cook and the idea that I can pass my knowledge on through my books, demos and now my new cookery school in Blacklion fills me with happiness.

But what I have noticed more than ever from talking to people in recent months is the incredible time pressure modern life has placed on us. Whether you're doing long hours at work or staying home to raise a brood – or combining the two! – the fact remains the same: we need to eat.

If we don't prepare and plan our meal times, we're likely to resort to quick and unhealthy fixes, which don't give us the nutrition and relaxation that meal times should bring – and as a result we're even more tired and less able to get back in the race!

That's why I've devised this cookbook. Every recipe in this book is doable and ready for the table in under an hour – most of them simply require 30 minutes. Since Amelda and I had our twins, Connor and Lucia, I have certainly changed the way I cook. I want recipes to turn to when time is tight and we want to eat … now! So here I'm sharing them with you: my ultimate fast and easy family recipes.

I recommend you start by incorporating one recipe into your weekly schedule: perhaps choose Crispy Tacos from the chicken section or Rib-eye Steak with Chimichurri from the beef section. My absolute favourite in this book is the Lamb Tagliata with Puy Lentil and Goat's Cheese Salad. If you make nothing else, try this! Then the following week try Pumpkin Pizza with Cashel Blue and Pickled Red Onion from the takeaway section: I guarantee you'll have it made before any delivery person could get to your house!

Soon you'll be on your way to planning weekly menus from the book and shopping accordingly. I promise you won't regret it. You'll be less frantic as you won't have to think about what to cook when you're hungry; you'll have lower shopping bills, as you'll only be buying what you need; and, most importantly, you'll be giving yourself what you need: good nutritious food that's satisfying and delicious, leaving you ready to get back to your busy life!

Enjoy!

Neven

SOUP

CARROT AND CUMIN SOUP

SERVES 4

2 tbsp rapeseed oil

1 large onion, chopped

450g (1lb) carrots, sliced

1 large potato, chopped

2 garlic cloves, crushed

2 tsp cumin seeds

1.2 litres (2 pints) vegetable or chicken stock (from cubes is fine)

400g (14oz) can cannellini or haricot beans, drained and rinsed

sea salt and freshly ground black pepper

swirl of cream or yoghurt, to garnish

chopped fresh flat-leaf parsley, to garnish

brown scones (page 236), to serve (optional)

This is a great soup to make on a cold winter evening when you want something warm and comforting in a bowl. I'd normally have all of the ingredients to hand, so there's no need for a special shop. The carrots could be replaced with pumpkin, butternut squash or sweet potatoes with great success.

Heat the oil in a large pan over a medium heat and fry the onion for 3–4 minutes, until softened but not coloured. Add the carrots, potato, garlic and cumin seeds and cook gently for 5–6 minutes, stirring until the carrots and potato begin to soften.

Add the stock to the pan and season to taste. Bring to the boil, then cover and simmer for 15 minutes, until the vegetables are tender. Blitz with a hand blender to a smooth purée.

Add the cannellini or haricot beans to the soup and allow them to warm through. Ladle into warmed bowls and add a swirl of cream or yoghurt to each one. Finish with a sprinkling of parsley and serve with the brown scones, if liked.

SWEET POTATO AND COCONUT SOUP WITH HAM

SERVES 6–8

900g (2lb) sweet potatoes, diced

2 tbsp sunflower oil

1 onion, finely chopped

1 celery stick, finely chopped

1 red chilli, halved, seeded and thinly sliced

1.25 litres (2¼ pints) vegetable or chicken stock

4 tsp tomato purée

400g (14oz) can coconut milk

225g (8oz) cooked, shredded ham hock

sea salt and freshly ground black pepper

handful of fresh coriander leaves, to garnish

crusty bread, to serve

I like to use leftover ham hock in this soup, but you could use shop-bought or even bacon would work well. This soup keeps well for 2–3 days in the fridge. It can also be frozen for up to 1 month, but it may need to be blitzed with a hand blender when reheating, as it may split.

Preheat the oven to 200°C (400°F/gas mark 6). Place the sweet potatoes in a baking tin, drizzle over 1 tablespoon of the sunflower oil and roast for 15 minutes, or until tender. Set aside.

Meanwhile, heat the remaining tablespoon of oil in a large pan over a medium heat. Add the onion, celery and chilli and sweat for 4 minutes, stirring occasionally. Add the roasted sweet potatoes with the stock and tomato purée, then bring to the boil. Reduce the heat and simmer for 5 minutes, until all of the vegetables are completely tender.

Reserve 3–4 tablespoons of the coconut milk as a garnish and pour the remainder into the pan with most of the shredded ham hock, again holding a little back to garnish. Cook for another few minutes, stirring constantly. Season to taste and ladle the soup into warmed bowls. Add a drizzle of the reserved coconut milk and scatter over the rest of the shredded ham hock and the coriander leaves to garnish. Serve hot with crusty bread on the side.

SPEEDY SOUPE DE POISSONS

SERVES 4

Every French town along the coast has a version of this soup, but none of them can be made as fast as this one! All the flavour comes from the prawns and the result is good enough to grace any dinner party.

Heat the oil in a large heavy-based pan over a medium heat. Add the shallots, carrot and celery and cook for a couple of minutes to soften. Tip in the prawns and sauté for another few minutes, until the shells have turned pink. Flambé with the Pernod and Cognac and then pour in the white wine and allow to bubble down.

Meanwhile, to make the rouille, crush the garlic with the salt and place in a small bowl. Whisk the paprika with the mayonnaise. Season with pepper and set aside until needed.

Stir the tomato purée into the pan with the stock and bring to the boil. Reduce the heat and simmer for about 5 minutes, until the vegetables are tender and the flavours have combined.

Carefully transfer the soup to a food processor. Blitz until smooth, then pass through a fine sieve into a clean pan. Whisk in the cream and correct the seasoning if necessary. Add the cooked prawns if using, and warm through but do not boil.

Ladle the soup into warmed shallow bowls and garnish each bowl with a prawn. Put a spoonful of the rouille on each croûte and then arrange 2 in each bowl. Add a drizzle of basil pesto, a sprinkling of the Gruyère and a grinding of black pepper to each one to serve.

2 tbsp olive oil

2 shallots, finely chopped

1 small carrot, finely chopped

1 celery stick, finely chopped

450g (1lb) raw tiger prawns
(with the shell on)

3 tbsp Pernod (anise liqueur)

2 tbsp Cognac

120ml (4fl oz) dry white wine

1 heaped tbsp tomato purée

300ml (½ pint) fish stock (chilled
from a carton is fine)

200ml (7fl oz) cream

4 cooked prawns, to
garnish (optional)

ROUILLE:

2 garlic cloves, peeled

½ tsp sea salt flakes

1 tsp hot paprika

4 tbsp mayonnaise

8 French bread croûtes
(or use shop-bought crostini)

2 tbsp basil pesto (shop-bought
or homemade), to serve

25g (1oz) Gruyère cheese, grated

sea salt and freshly ground
black pepper

ASPARAGUS SOUP WITH BELLINGHAM BLUE AND CROUTONS

SERVES 4–6

675g (1½lb) bunch of asparagus, woody ends removed

50g (2oz) butter

2 large shallots, finely chopped

1 potato, finely diced

900ml (1½ pints) chicken or vegetable stock

175g (6oz) Bellingham Blue cheese, crumbled

100ml (3½fl oz) cream, plus extra to garnish

sea salt and freshly ground black pepper

crunchy croutons, to garnish

extra virgin olive oil, to garnish

Bellingham Blue has to be one of the most divine cheeses in the world. Its layers of blue-veined creaminess are both seductively rich and delicate, making it a perfect partner for asparagus. Here I've served the soup hot, but it is also delicious chilled.

Cut 5cm (2in) of the tips off the asparagus stalks and simmer them very gently in a pan of boiling salted water for 3–4 minutes, until just tender. Drain well and refresh under cold running water. Set aside. Roughly chop the remaining stalks.

Meanwhile, heat the butter in a large pan over a medium heat and add the shallots, potato and chopped asparagus stalks. Cover and cook gently for 10 minutes, until softened but not coloured, stirring once or twice. Pour in the stock, season to taste and bring to the boil. Reduce the heat and simmer for 10 minutes, until the potatoes are completely tender and the soup has thickened slightly.

Purée the soup with a hand-held blender. Whisk in most of the Bellingham Blue cheese, reserving some for a garnish, and the cream. Season to taste and heat gently, being careful not to let it boil. Serve hot or chilled, ladled into bowls and garnished with the reserved asparagus tips, the rest of the Bellingham Blue cheese and a sprinkling of croutons. Drizzle over a little extra virgin olive oil to finish and add a grinding of black pepper.

SPINACH AND WATERCRESS SOUP WITH A POACHED EGG

SERVES 4

1 tbsp white wine vinegar

4 medium eggs

25g (1oz) butter

1 onion, finely chopped

1 garlic clove, finely chopped

300g (11oz) watercress, tough stalks removed, plus extra sprigs to garnish

100g (4oz) baby spinach leaves

500ml (18fl oz) vegetable or chicken stock

225g (8oz) ice cubes

2 tbsp crème fraîche

sea salt and freshly ground black pepper

This wonderfully light soup is perfect to serve a vegetarian if made with vegetable stock. Using the ice cubes might seem strange, but it's a great way to keep the vibrant green colour, locking in all those important vitamins and minerals.

To prepare the poached eggs, heat a large pan with 2.25 litres (4 pints) of water. Add the white wine vinegar and bring to the boil. Break each egg into the water where it is bubbling, then reduce the heat and simmer gently for 3 minutes, until the eggs are just cooked through but the yolks are still soft. Remove with a slotted spoon and plunge into a bowl of iced water. Set the pot of water aside to reuse later.

Meanwhile, melt the butter in a large pan over a medium heat. Add the onion and garlic and cook for 2–3 minutes, until softened but not coloured. Increase the heat to high, then add the watercress and a pinch of salt. Cover with a lid and cook for 30 seconds. Add the spinach and cook for 1–2 minutes, until just wilted, stirring.

Pour in the stock and simmer for 2–3 minutes but no longer or you will lose the wonderful vibrant colour. Remove from the heat and add the ice to help the soup cool down quickly. Blitz with a hand-held blender until smooth and season to taste.

To reheat the poached eggs when you are ready to serve, bring the large pan of salted water to the boil. Reheat the soup and season to taste. Add the poached eggs to the boiling salted water and cook for 1 minute to warm through. Ladle the soup into warmed bowls. Loosen the crème fraîche with a little water and add a swirl to each bowl. Top each bowl with a drained poached egg and a light grinding of black pepper. Garnish with the watercress sprigs to serve.

STARTERS

SMOKED DUCK SALAD WITH STRAWBERRY DRESSING

SERVES 4

120g (4½ oz) packet sliced smoked duck breast (Silver Hill, if possible)

1 large orange, flesh cut into segments

100g (4oz) strawberries, hulled and diced into cubes

50g (2oz) mixed salad leaves

3 tbsp toasted flaked almonds

STRAWBERRY DRESSING:

finely grated rind of ½ orange

3 tbsp rapeseed oil

2 tbsp strawberry vinegar

1 tsp runny honey

1 tsp snipped fresh chives

sea salt and freshly ground black pepper

This is a lovely starter that proves a little can go a long way. You'll only need a 120g (4½ oz) packet of smoked duck, which is now available in large supermarkets and good delis. Otherwise it works well with Ummera smoked chicken, depending on your preference.

To make the dressing, whisk the orange rind in a bowl with the rapeseed oil, strawberry vinegar, honey and chives and season to taste.

Divide the smoked duck between the plates. Arrange the orange segments between each duck slice. Sprinkle the diced strawberries over the duck and oranges. Mix the salad leaves with the dressing and arrange in the centre of the duck slices. Drizzle any remaining dressing over the top, then scatter over the toasted almonds to serve.

COOLEENEY CHEESE FILO PARCELS WITH CRANBERRY CONFIT

SERVES 6

75g (3oz) butter

270g (10 oz) packet filo pastry, thawed if frozen (6 individual sheets)

2 x 175g (6oz) rounds of Cooleeney cheese, each cut into 6 wedges

lightly dressed spinach, watercress and rocket salad, to serve

CRANBERRY CONFIT:

100g (4oz) dried cranberries

100g (4oz) fresh cranberries

juice of 2 oranges

75g (3oz) light muscovado sugar

1 small red onion, finely chopped

4 tbsp white wine vinegar

1 tsp chopped fresh rosemary

Using dried cranberries as well as fresh gives this confit a much more concentrated, intense flavour. If you are not short of time, these filo parcels can be made up to a day in advance and kept covered in the fridge with clingfilm until needed.

Preheat the oven to 200°C (400°F/gas mark 6). Line a large baking sheet with parchment paper.

Melt the butter in a small pan or in the microwave. Place the 6 filo pastry sheets on top of each other and cut in half down the length and in thirds across the width to make 36 rectangles. Layer the filo rectangles into 12 stacks of 3 rectangles, slightly overlapping the points to create a star shape and brushing with the melted butter as you go. Place one of the Cooleeney cheese wedges into the centre of each star. Gather the pastry edges up around the filling, pinching the tops together to form little 'money bags'. Place the filo purses on the lined baking sheet and bake for 16–18 minutes, until crisp and golden brown.

Meanwhile, make the cranberry confit. Bring the dried and fresh cranberries to the boil in a pan with the orange juice, sugar, onion, vinegar and rosemary. Continue to boil for 1–2 minutes, until the sugar has dissolved, stirring regularly. Reduce the heat and simmer for another 10–15 minutes, until the fresh cranberries have popped and most of the liquid has evaporated.

Arrange 2 of the Cooleeney cheese filo parcels on each plate with a small pile of the salad leaves and add a spoonful of the cranberry confit to each one to serve.

LOBSTER AND MANGO COCKTAIL

SERVES 4

This starter is a spectacular combination and looks amazing served in a Martini cocktail glass. It can be made a couple of hours in advance, so it's an excellent starter if you are entertaining special guests. I'm going to serve it on Christmas Day this year and I think it will go down a treat!

Shred the lettuce and arrange in the bottom of 4 Martini glasses. Peel the mango and cut into dice, discarding the stone. Scatter over the lettuce in a neat layer.

Place the mayonnaise in a liquidiser with the avocado and tomato relish and blend until smooth. Transfer to a squeezy bottle.

Arrange the lobster meat on the mango and pipe over the avocado mayonnaise. Add a good grinding of black pepper and a light dusting of smoked paprika. Garnish each one with sprigs of micro coriander and add a lime wedge to serve.

1 Baby Gem lettuce, outer leaves discarded

½ small, ripe mango

100ml (3½fl oz) mayonnaise

1 ripe avocado, peeled, stone removed and roughly chopped

1 tbsp tomato relish (such as Ballymaloe)

400g (14oz) fresh white lobster meat, well picked over

sea salt and freshly ground black pepper

smoked paprika, to garnish

fresh micro coriander sprigs, to garnish

lime wedges, to serve

CRISPY GOAT'S CHEESE WITH APPLE AND HAZELNUT SALAD

SERVES 4

25g (1oz) fresh white breadcrumbs

1 tbsp finely chopped fresh flat-leaf parsley

1 tbsp sesame seeds

2 tsp very finely chopped skinned, toasted hazelnuts

1 egg

25g (1oz) plain flour

150g (5oz) log of Corleggy goat's cheese, cut into 4 slices

sunflower oil, for deep-frying

SALAD:

2 crisp Irish eating apples

juice of 1 lemon

50g (2oz) rocket leaves

2 tablespoons extra virgin olive oil

50g (20z) skinned, toasted hazelnuts, roughly chopped

sea salt and freshly ground black pepper

If you prefer to bake the goat's cheese, simply cook it in an oven preheated to 180°C (350°F/gas mark 4) for another 5–10 minutes, until warmed through and soft. Look for Irish apples in the supermarket, particularly when they are in season, and if they're not there, ask the manager why! Apples are one of our few indigenous fruits and there is no excuse for the shops not supporting Irish farmers.

To prepare the crispy goat's cheese, mix the breadcrumbs with the parsley, sesame seeds and chopped hazelnuts in a shallow dish and season to taste. In a separate dish, beat the egg and season lightly. Season the flour and place in another shallow dish.

Lightly coat the goat's cheese in the seasoned flour, then dip each slice into the beaten egg, gently shaking off any excess. Place in the breadcrumb mixture so that they are completely coated. Set on a baking sheet lined with parchment paper and place in the fridge for at least 10 minutes to firm up.

Preheat the oven to 180°C (350°F/gas mark 4).

Heat the oil in a deep-sided pan or deep-fat fryer to 180°C (350°F) and cook the breaded goat's cheese for 1–2 minutes, until golden brown. Carefully remove from the oil and transfer to a plate lined with kitchen paper to drain off any excess oil. Arrange back on the lined baking sheet and place in the oven for 3–4 minutes, until heated through but still holding their shape.

Meanwhile, make the apple and hazelnut salad. Using a mandolin or a very sharp knife, cut the apples into wafer-thin slices and toss in the lemon juice to prevent discoloration. Cover each plate with a layer of slightly overlapping apple slices and add a small mound of the rocket, then drizzle with olive oil. Put the crispy goat's cheese into the centre of each plate and scatter over the hazelnuts to serve.

SMOKED TROUT AND CREAM CHEESE ROLL WITH PICKLED CUCUMBER SALAD

SERVES 4

200g (7oz) carton Kilbeg soft cream cheese

1 tbsp finely diced radish

1 tbsp snipped fresh chives

2 tsp creamed horseradish

1 tsp finely diced cucumber, peeled and seeded

1 tsp prepared English mustard

3 x 200g (7oz) packets cold smoked trout slices (such as Goatsbridge)

PICKLED CUCUMBER SALAD:

4 tbsp rice wine vinegar

2 tbsp caster sugar

½ small cucumber, peeled, halved and seeded

trout caviar (optional), to garnish

fresh tiny dill sprigs, to garnish

salt and freshly ground black pepper

This can also be served as a canapé or it would make an excellent starter for a dinner party, as it can all be prepared well in advance. You could also use smoked salmon, but I particularly like the taste of smoked trout, which is more subtle and often less salty than smoked salmon.

To make the pickled cucumber salad, place the vinegar in a bowl and stir in the sugar and a pinch of salt to dissolve. Cut the cucumber into thin slices and toss in the brine to coat. Cover with clingfilm and set aside for at least 10 minutes.

Meanwhile, mix together the cream cheese, diced radish, chives, horseradish, diced cucumber, mustard and a little pepper in a small bowl. Reserve 12 of the best slices of the trout. Finely chop the remainder and add to the cream cheese mixture.

Lay 6 slices of smoked trout on a large piece of clingfilm, then spoon half of the cream cheese mixture down the centre. Roll the smoked trout over to enclose the filling and make a sausage shape. Wrap tightly in the clingfilm and chill for 10 minutes while you use the rest of the ingredients to make another roll.

When ready to serve, trim off the ends of each smoked trout and cream cheese roll and then cut into 6 even-sized slices. Arrange 3 slices on each plate and garnish with a line of the trout caviar, if using. Put a small mound of the pickled cucumber salad to the side of each one and garnish with the dill sprigs to serve.

SALADS

BRUSSELS SPROUT AND DRIED CRANBERRY SALAD

SERVES 4

250g (9oz) Brussels sprouts, well trimmed

50g (2oz) dried cranberries

2 tbsp snipped fresh chives

25g (1oz) toasted flaked almonds

FRENCH DRESSING:

1 tbsp white wine vinegar

pinch of caster sugar

4 tbsp extra virgin olive oil

1 small garlic clove, crushed

½ tsp Dijon mustard

sea salt and freshly ground black pepper

This is an excellent way of serving Brussels sprouts that everyone will enjoy. It lasts very well in the fridge, so it's a great dish to make around the festive season.

To make the French dressing, place the vinegar in a screw-top jar and add the sugar and a good pinch of salt, then shake until the sugar has dissolved. Add the oil to the jar with the garlic and mustard and shake again until a thick emulsion has formed. Season to taste and set aside until needed.

Cut the Brussels sprouts on a mandolin so that they are very finely shredded. Fold in enough of the French dressing to lightly coat and then fold in the cranberries and chives. Serve at once scattered with the almonds or keep in the fridge until needed.

LITTLE GEM SALAD WITH CASHEL BLUE DRESSING

SERVES 4

This salad looks amazing simply by cutting the Little Gem lettuce hearts in half. They can be served raw or griddled, depending on what you fancy. Cutting them this way also has the added bonus of making it easy to catch the dressing in little puddles between the layers, making your salad perfectly dressed from start to finish. I just love it with cold roast beef or with leftover cooked or smoked chicken.

Trim down the Little Gem lettuces and use the outer leaves for sandwiches. Cut the lettuce hearts in half and arrange 3 on each plate.

To make the dressing, crumble the Cashel Blue cheese into a bowl and whisk in the soured cream and milk to make a dressing consistency. Add the Worcestershire sauce and lemon juice to taste and then season with salt and pepper. Drizzle the dressing all over the Little Gem lettuce hearts to serve.

6 Little Gem lettuces

CASHEL BLUE DRESSING:
150g (5oz) Cashel Blue cheese, rind removed
120ml (4fl oz) soured cream
4 tbsp milk
few drops of Worcestershire sauce
squeeze of lemon juice
sea salt and freshly ground black pepper

GRIDDLED PEAR, ENDIVE, PECORINO AND WALNUT SALAD

SERVES 4

2 x 400g (14oz) can pear halves
in syrup, drained

1 tbsp olive oil

50g (2oz) shelled walnut halves

1 Belgian endive

1 small head frisée lettuce,
well trimmed

25g (1oz) Pecorino cheese shavings

DRESSING:

2 tbsp mayonnaise

2 tbsp buttermilk

1 small garlic clove, crushed

squeeze of lemon juice

2 tsp chopped fresh
flat-leaf parsley

2 tsp snipped fresh chives

sea salt and freshly ground
black pepper

This is a wonderful salad that is perfect to serve in the autumn or winter. You could use fresh pears and poach them in syrup first yourself, but when time is tight, canned pears are a great option.

Heat a cast iron griddle pan until smoking hot. Cut each pear half in half again and pat dry with kitchen paper, then brush with the oil. Add to the griddle pan and quickly char on both cut sides. Transfer to a plate. Toast the walnuts on the pan until lightly golden, then leave to cool and roughly chop.

To make the dressing, put the mayonnaise and buttermilk in a bowl and whisk in the garlic, lemon juice, parsley and chives. Season to taste.

Trim the endive and separate out into leaves. Remove the outer leaves from the frisée lettuce and break up the pale yellow leaves. Divide the endive leaves among 4 plates and sit a piece of pear on top of each one, topped with a sprinkling of chopped walnuts. Scatter over the frisée and Pecorino cheese and drizzle over the dressing to serve.

WATERMELON AND FETA SALAD WITH TOASTED PUMPKIN SEEDS

SERVES 4

2 tbsp pumpkin seeds

1 tbsp green peppercorns, rinsed and drained if in brine

1kg (2¼lb) watermelon

120g (4½oz) feta cheese

handful of fresh flat-leaf parsley leaves

small handfull of fresh mint leaves

finely grated rind and juice of 2 limes

2 tbsp olive oil

This recipe also works well with Galia or Honeydew melon if watermelon is not in season. You can pare it down to the essential contrasts and serve no more than a plate of chunky watermelon sprinkled with feta and toasted pumpkin seeds that gets drizzled with lime juice at the last minute. Once made, I promise you that it will become a regular favourite on your summer table.

Preheat the oven to 180°C (350°F/gas mark 4). Toast the pumpkin seeds in a small baking dish for 5–6 minutes, until lightly coloured.

Crack the peppercorns gently between your fingers or with the flat of a knife.

Deseed the watermelon and cut the flesh into medium-sized chunks (discard the rind). Chop the feta into small cubes and place in a bowl with the watermelon, herbs and the pumpkin seeds. Add the lime rind and juice with the olive oil and toss gently to combine.

Pile a mound of the watermelon and feta salad onto plates. Scatter over the green peppercorns and serve chilled or at room temperature.

RED CABBAGE SALAD

SERVES 4

½ small red cabbage

½ small red onion

1 raw beetroot, peeled

1 red-skinned eating apple

50g (2oz) shelled walnuts or pecans, toasted and roughly chopped

25g (1oz) currants

4 tbsp extra virgin olive oil

2 tbsp red wine vinegar

2 tsp light muscovado sugar

fresh flat-leaf parsley leaves, to garnish

sea salt and freshly ground black pepper

This red cabbage salad is delicious with any type of game, particularly venison steaks. It would also be lovely as part of a buffet for a barbecue and makes a nice change from traditional coleslaw.

Finely shred the cabbage on a mandolin. Finely grate the red onion and add to the cabbage, then grate the beetroot and apple on a box grater and add in with the nuts, currants, oil, vinegar and sugar. Stir well to combine and season to taste. Cover with clingfilm and set aside at room temperature for 10 minutes to allow the flavours to develop.

To serve, remove the clingfilm from the red cabbage salad and give it a good stir. Use as required and garnish with a few leaves of flat-leaf parsley.

BEEF

MINCED BEEF AND ONION PIE WITH SOUFFLÉ CROUTON TOPPING

SERVES 4

2 tbsp rapeseed oil

1 large onion, chopped

1 large carrot, chopped

1 celery stick, chopped

1 tsp chopped fresh rosemary

400g (14oz) lean minced beef

1 tbsp Worcestershire sauce

1 tsp Marmite

2 tsp plain flour

1 tsp English mustard

200ml (7fl oz) beef stock
(from a cube is fine)

buttered peas, to serve

SOUFFLÉ TOPPING:

75g (3oz) butter

75g (3oz) mature Cheddar
cheese, grated

3 tbsp cream

1 large egg white

150g (5oz) small white bread
cubes (no crusts and from
stale bread)

sea salt and freshly ground
black pepper

This is a great one-pot (or should I say frying pan) meal. It has plenty of flavour and is topped with a fantastic bread and soufflé-style topping that uses up bread that's past its sell by date.

Preheat the oven to 200°C (400°F/gas mark 6).

Heat the oil in a 23cm (9in) ovenproof frying pan over a medium heat and sauté the onion, carrot and celery for a couple of minutes, until they are just beginning to soften. Stir in the rosemary with the minced beef, breaking up any lumps with a wooden spoon. Add the Worcestershire sauce, Marmite, flour and mustard and cook for 1 minute, stirring. Pour in the stock and bring to a simmer, then cook for another 5 minutes to cook out the flour, stirring occasionally.

Meanwhile, prepare the soufflé topping. Place the butter, Cheddar cheese and cream in a small pan and melt over a low heat until runny – don't worry if the mixture looks a bit curdled; this is normal. Whisk the egg white until stiff and then fold into the melted cheese mixture. Season to taste and carefully fold in the bread cubes until evenly coated.

Quickly spoon the soufflé topping over the minced beef base and transfer the pan to the oven for 15 minutes, until the soufflé topping is golden brown and bubbling. Serve straight to the table with a separate bowl of buttered peas and allow everyone to help themselves.

RIB-EYE STEAK WITH CHIMICHURRI

SERVES 4

450g (1lb) baby new potatoes

4 x 200g (7oz) rib-eye steaks, well trimmed

1 tbsp olive oil

fresh coriander leaves, to garnish

fresh cherry tomato and red onion salad, to serve

CHIMICHURRI SAUCE:

4 spring onions, trimmed and chopped

4 garlic cloves, peeled

1 red chilli, seeded

1 bunch fresh flat-leaf parsley

3 tbsp red wine vinegar

2 heaped tsp dried oregano

pinch of hot paprika

pinch of ground cumin

sea salt and freshly ground black pepper

Chimichurri is a green sauce that is traditionally served with barbecued or grilled meat in Argentina. Rib-eye is my favourite cut of beef for a steak, as it has the perfect balance between flavour and value for money.

Place the new potatoes in a steamer and sprinkle over a little salt, then cook for about 15 minutes, until tender.

Meanwhile, heat a barbecue or cast-iron griddle pan. Rub the steaks with a little olive oil and season with salt and pepper. Place on the barbecue or griddle pan for 3–4 minutes on each side for medium rare – leave them on a little longer if you prefer your meat more well done. Transfer to a warm plate and loosely cover with foil. Set aside to rest for about 5 minutes.

To make the chimichurri sauce, put the spring onions, garlic, chilli, parsley, vinegar, oregano, paprika, cumin and 3 tablespoons of water in a liquidiser and blend to a smooth sauce. Divide among 4 dipping bowls.

Carve the steaks on the diagonal and arrange a steak on each platter or warmed plate. Garnish with the coriander leaves and add the cherry tomato and red onion salad and a dipping bowl of the chimichurri sauce. Serve with a separate dish of the steamed new potatoes.

BEEF STROGANOFF WITH FLUFFY RICE AND DILL PICKLE SHAVINGS

SERVES 4

Traditionally this was served with buttered noodles, not unlike tagliatelle, but it is so much nicer with fluffy rice. The soured cream is not strictly necessary and regular cream will work just as well.

Toss the flour and paprika together in a shallow dish and add some seasoning and then use to coat the steak. Heat half the butter and oil in a frying pan over a high heat. Add the steak and stir-fry for 4–5 minutes, until sealed and lightly browned. Tip onto a plate and set aside.

Reheat the pan over a medium heat. Add the rest of the butter and oil and then add the shallot. Sauté for 2–3 minutes, until softened but not coloured. Increase the heat to high and add the mushrooms to the pan with the garlic. Season to taste and continue to sauté for another 2–3 minutes, until tender.

Add the white wine vinegar and allow to bubble right down, then add the stock, wine, tomato purée and mustard, stirring to combine. Tip the sautéed beef with any juices back into the pan, then bring to the boil. Reduce the heat and simmer gently for about 5 minutes, until the sauce has reduced by half, stirring occasionally.

Stir the soured cream into the pan and return to the boil, then reduce the heat again and simmer gently for a couple of minutes, until the sauce has thickened and slightly reduced. Divide the fluffy rice between warmed plates and spoon over the beef stroganoff. Add dill pickle shavings and a good grinding of black pepper. Serve at once.

1 tbsp plain flour

2 tsp sweet paprika

450g (1lb) sirloin steak, cut into thin strips

25g (1oz) butter

2 tbsp sunflower oil

1 large shallot, finely chopped

150g (5oz) button mushrooms, halved

1 garlic clove, crushed

1 tbsp white wine vinegar

150ml (¼ pint) chicken stock

4 tbsp white wine

2 tsp tomato purée

1 tsp Dijon mustard

150ml (¼ pint) soured cream

sea salt and freshly ground black pepper

fluffy rice, to serve

dill pickle shavings, to serve

STEAK WITH ROASTED PEPPERCORN SAUCE

SERVES 4

1 tbsp white peppercorns

1 tbsp black peppercorns

4 x 175g (6oz) striploin steaks
(preferably dry-aged)

2 tsp rapeseed oil

50g (2oz) butter

2 shallots, finely chopped

85ml (3fl oz) fresh beef stock
(from a carton is fine)

2 tsp Worcestershire sauce

6 tbsp cream

2 tsp Dijon mustard

1 tsp drained green peppercorns
in brine, rinsed

2 tbsp whiskey (such as Kilbeggan)

salt, to taste

garlic mashed potatoes (page 164),
to serve

steamed broccoli, to serve

This classic dish is so delicious, it's no wonder that it has stood the test of time. Use the best dry-aged steaks you can afford and make sure you give them plenty of time to rest before serving them to allow all the juices to settle.

Dry roast the peppercorns for a couple of minutes, until aromatic. Transfer to a pestle and mortar and lightly crush down, then tip onto a flat plate. Pat the steaks dry with kitchen paper and press the mixed peppercorns onto both sides of the steaks using your hands.

Heat the oil in a large heavy-based frying pan over a high heat. Add the steaks and cook for 2 minutes on each side, then reduce the heat, add half the butter and cook the steaks for 5 minutes more, turning once, depending on how rare you like it. Transfer the steaks to a plate, season with salt and set aside in a warm place to rest while you make the sauce.

Pour away any excess fat from the pan, add the remaining butter and fry the shallots for a few minutes, until softened but not browned. Add the stock and Worcestershire sauce and cook rapidly, scraping the bottom of the pan with a wooden spoon to release any sediment. Stir in the cream, mustard and green peppercorns, then season to taste with salt and just warm through. Heat the whiskey in a ladle over a flame and wait until it ignites, then pour it over the cream, stirring to combine. Simmer for 1–2 minutes to warm through.

Arrange the steaks on warmed plates, stirring any juices from the rested steaks into the peppercorn sauce. Drizzle the sauce over the steaks and serve with the garlic mashed potatoes and steamed broccoli.

STEAK SANDWICH WITH CARAMELISED ONIONS

SERVES 4

3 tbsp olive oil

2 large red onions, thinly sliced and separated into rings

1 tbsp light muscovado sugar

1 tbsp balsamic vinegar

4 x 175g (6oz) thin-cut rump or sirloin steak

1 small ciabatta loaf, cut into 4 pieces

8 tbsp mayonnaise

2 tsp Dijon mustard

2 tsp wholegrain mustard

4 ripe tomatoes, sliced

50g (2oz) wild rocket

sea salt and freshly ground black pepper

There are times when you want something tasty and delicious but just don't feel like cooking a full meal. This is one of those dishes you'll find yourself cooking again and again. If you want to make it even more substantial, try serving it with crispy, fat chips and watch how quickly the plates are cleared!

Heat 2 tablespoons of the oil in a large frying pan over a medium heat and preheat the grill. Fry the onions for 10 minutes, until softened, stirring occasionally. Sprinkle over the sugar and balsamic vinegar and cook for another 2–3 minutes, until the sugar has dissolved and is slightly syrupy, stirring continuously. Keep warm.

Meanwhile, heat a griddle pan over a high heat. Rub the remaining tablespoon of oil into the steaks and season them generously. Add them to the heated pan and cook over a high heat for 3–4 minutes on each side for well done, or according to taste.

Split each piece of the ciabatta loaf in half and arrange on the grill rack, cut side up. Place under the grill until lightly toasted. Mix the mayonnaise in a small bowl with the mustards.

Place a piece of the toasted ciabatta on each warmed serving plate. Add a good smear of the mustard mayonnaise and then arrange a layer of the tomato slices on it. Season to taste and add the rocket. Place the steak on top and add the reserved caramelised onions. Dollop over the rest of the mustard mayonnaise to serve.

CHICKEN

CRISPY CHICKEN TACOS

SERVES 4

4 x 100g (4oz) skinless, boneless chicken breast fillets

olive oil, for brushing

2 tsp smoked paprika

8 corn tortillas

150g (5oz) Cheddar cheese, grated

400g (14oz) can kidney beans, rinsed and drained

4 spring onions, finely chopped

2 ripe tomatoes, finely chopped

good handful of fresh coriander leaves

juice of 1 lime

sea salt and freshly ground black pepper

lime wedges, to serve

soured cream, to serve

This is a real favourite in the Maguire household. It's a great recipe for a sudden influx of hungry people – so fast and easy to prepare. Everybody can help. If you haven't got smoked paprika, try using Cajun seasoning instead.

Heat a non-stick frying pan over a high heat. Brush the chicken fillets with the oil and sprinkle over the smoked paprika, then season to taste. Add to the heated pan, reduce the heat to medium and cook for 4–5 minutes on each side, until just tender and cooked through. Remove from the heat and leave to rest for 5 minutes, then cut into thin slices.

Wipe out the pan and put it back on a medium heat. Brush a corn tortilla with oil and place in the pan, oiled side down. Place some of the cheese on one half of the tortilla and then add some of the chicken on top, followed by a scattering of kidney beans, spring onions, tomatoes and coriander leaves. Add a squeeze of lime juice and fold over to enclose the filling.

Cook the tortilla for 1–2 minutes on each side, until crisp and lightly golden. Repeat with the remaining ingredients and arrange on warmed plates. Serve with the lime wedges and a separate small dish of soured cream.

SPEEDY COQ AU VIN

SERVES 4

25g (1oz) plain flour

450g (1lb) skinless, boneless chicken thighs, well trimmed and quartered

2 tbsp olive oil

knob of butter

175g (6oz) button onions or small shallots, halved

175g (6oz) button mushrooms, trimmed

100g (4oz) pancetta (streaky bacon lardons)

450ml (¾ pint) chicken stock (from a cube is fine)

150ml (¼ pint) red wine

2 tsp Worcestershire sauce

1 tsp chopped fresh thyme, plus extra leaves to garnish

2 tbsp chopped fresh flat-leaf parsley

sea salt and freshly ground black pepper

garlic mashed potatoes (page 164), to serve

steamed French beans, to serve

This coq au vin is made with chicken thighs, which have a wonderful succulent flavour, but you could use chicken breasts if you prefer. I love it with the garlic mashed potatoes, but buttered noodles would also work well and take much less time to prepare.

Season the flour and toss the chicken thigh pieces in it until lightly coated, shaking off any excess. Heat the oil in a large sauté pan over a medium-high heat and tip in the dusted chicken. Sauté for 3–4 minutes, stirring occasionally, until just beginning to brown. Add the butter and toss until evenly coated, then add the onions or shallots, mushrooms and pancetta and cook for 3–4 minutes.

Pour the stock into the pan with the wine and Worcestershire sauce, then add the thyme. Bring to the boil, then reduce the heat and simmer gently for about 15 minutes, until the chicken and vegetables are cooked through and the sauce is slightly reduced and thickened. Stir in the parsley and season to taste.

Place the garlic mashed potatoes on warmed plates and spoon over the coq au vin. Garnish with some thyme leaves and serve with the steamed French beans.

VIETNAMESE PHO WITH CHICKEN DUMPLINGS AND PAK CHOY

SERVES 4

This is a wonderful soup/stew to serve to someone who is feeling a bit under the weather. It might sound exotic, but pak choy is now grown very successfully by Irish farmers. Look for it in the supermarket and make sure you check the label to see where it was grown.

Pour the chicken stock into a large heavy-based pan. Add the ginger, garlic, star anise, kaffir lime leaves and the cinnamon stick. Roughly chop 1 of the chillies and add to the stock. Bring to a gentle simmer and allow to gently bubble away for 20 minutes.

Meanwhile, seed and finely chop the remaining chilli and put into a food processor with the minced chicken, spring onions, 2 tablespoons of the fish sauce, the coriander and the lime rind. Blend until mixed together. I use the pulse button so the mixture keeps some texture. Roll into 20 bite-sized balls.

Heat a large frying pan over a medium-high heat. Add the rapeseed oil and then the chicken balls. Fry for 6–8 minutes, until golden brown and just cooked through. Keep them moving all the time to ensure they colour evenly.

Pour boiling water over the noodles and leave to stand for 10 minutes, then drain and set aside. Strain the stock to remove the herbs and spices, then return to the pan with the remaining 2 tablespoons of the fish sauce and the pak choy. Bring to a gentle simmer, allowing the pak choy to just wilt.

Just before serving, add the chicken balls to the simmering stock. Warm deep serving bowls and divide the noodles between them. Pour over the soup and chicken balls, ensuring you divide them evenly between the bowls. Finally, garnish with beansprouts, spring onions, chilli, if using, coriander leaves and lime wedges to serve.

1.5 litres (2½ pints) chicken stock

2.5cm (1in) piece root ginger, peeled and finely grated

2 garlic cloves, finely grated

4 star anise

4 kaffir lime leaves (fresh, dried or frozen)

1 cinnamon stick

2 red chillies, seeds removed if preferred (depending on how hot you like it)

450g (1lb) minced chicken

4 spring onions, very finely sliced

4 tbsp Thai fish sauce (nam pla)

2 tbsp chopped fresh coriander

finely grated rind of 1 lime

1 tbsp rapeseed oil

150g (5oz) vermicelli rice noodles

150g (5oz) pak choy, roughly chopped

TO SERVE:

75g (3oz) fresh beansprouts

4 spring onions, finely sliced

1 red chilli, thinly sliced (optional)

handful of picked fresh coriander leaves

1 lime, cut into wedges

CHICKEN AND CHICKPEA TAGINE WITH HONEY AND GINGER

SERVES 4

8 large skinless, boneless chicken thighs or 4 skinless, boneless breasts

1 tbsp clear honey

1 tsp ground ginger

1 tsp cayenne pepper

½ tsp paprika

½ tsp ground turmeric

½ tsp ground cinnamon

3 tbsp olive oil

1 small red onion, finely sliced

2 garlic cloves, finely chopped

400g (14oz) can chickpeas, drained and rinsed

2 ripe tomatoes, peeled, seeded and chopped

1 red pepper, seeded and thinly sliced into strips

2 tbsp tomato purée

450ml (¾ pint) chicken stock

juice of ½ lemon

2 tbsp chopped fresh coriander

1 tbsp chopped fresh mint, plus extra leaves to garnish

sea salt and freshly ground black pepper

steamed green herby couscous, to serve (optional)

The combination of spicy chicken, tomatoes and chickpeas here is really successful, and the best thing about it is that it all gets cooked in the one pot, so there's very little washing up. I've suggested serving it with steamed couscous, but bulghur wheat, or if you want to be really trendy, quinoa, would be equally delicious. And don't just dress the couscous with lemon. In Morocco they use everything from sultanas to bananas and/or toasted nuts, as the essence of their cooking is the exquisite combination of fruit and nuts.

Trim down the chicken and cut into bite-sized pieces. Place in a bowl with the honey, spices and 1 tablespoon of the oil. Season generously, then stir well to combine and set aside for at least 5 minutes to allow the flavours to develop.

Meanwhile, heat the remaining 2 tablespoons of oil over a medium heat in a large sauté pan with a lid, then sauté the onion and garlic for 4–5 minutes, until softened and just beginning to brown. Add the marinated chicken and sauté for 1–2 minutes, until just sealed and lightly browned.

Add the chickpeas to the pan with half of the tomatoes and the red pepper, tomato purée and stock, then bring to the boil. Reduce the heat, cover and simmer for 10–12 minutes, until the chicken is completely tender and the sauce has slightly thickened, stirring occasionally. Season to taste.

Stir the remaining tomatoes into the pan and season to taste again, then add the lemon juice, coriander and mint. Stir to combine and arrange on warmed plates with the herby green couscous and scatter over the mint leaves to garnish.

CRISPY CHICKEN THIGHS WITH BRAISED PUY LENTILS

SERVES 4

3 tbsp olive oil

8 boneless chicken thighs, well trimmed (skin on)

2 carrots, finely diced

1 leek, trimmed and finely diced

1 celery stick, finely diced

2 x 400g (14oz) cans Puy lentils, rinsed and drained

½ tsp fresh thyme leaves

300ml (½ pint) chicken stock

splash of balsamic vinegar

pinch of sugar

2 tbsp chopped fresh flat-leaf parsley, plus extra leaves to garnish

sea salt and freshly ground black pepper

Don't be tempted to touch the chicken thighs or shake the pan while they are cooking – just leave them alone and you will get the most fantastic crisp skin and succulent flesh. Once made, these lentils will keep for up to 5 days in a bowl covered with clingfilm in the fridge. It's a great winter warmer that you can have on the table in no time at all.

Heat 1 tablespoon of the oil in a frying pan over a medium heat. Season the chicken thighs all over. Add the chicken to the heated pan, skin side down, then reduce the heat to very low and cook for about 20 minutes, until the skin is crispy and browned and the flesh has almost completely cooked through. Turn them over and cook for another 4–5 minutes, until completely cooked through and tender.

Meanwhile, heat the remaining 2 tablespoons of oil in a large pan over a medium heat and sweat the carrots, leek and celery for about 10 minutes, until softened but not coloured. Stir in the lentils and thyme and then pour in the stock. Season to taste and add the balsamic vinegar and sugar, then simmer for a few minutes, until you have a loose sauce and the vegetables are completely tender.

Stir the parsley into the braised lentils and season to taste, then spoon into warmed wide-rimmed bowls and arrange the crispy chicken thighs on top. Garnish with the parsley leaves to serve.

LAMB

GRIDDLED LAMB CHOPS WITH COURGETTES AND LEMON

SERVES 4

2 garlic cloves, crushed

2 tbsp olive oil

2 tsp clear honey

1 tsp chopped fresh oregano

8 lamb chops

4 small courgettes, sliced
on the diagonal

450g (1lb) baby new potatoes

few sprigs of fresh mint

4 lemon wedges

100g (4oz) goat's curd or soft
goat's cheese

sea salt and freshly ground
black pepper

This recipe would also be perfect on the barbecue on a nice summer evening when you don't want to spend too much time cooking. If you don't fancy the goat's curd or soft goat's cheese, try serving it with some tzatziki.

Mix together the garlic, oil, honey, oregano and seasoning in a shallow non-metallic dish. Add the lamb chops and courgette slices and mix until evenly combined. Set aside for 10 minutes at room temperature to allow the flavours to develop.

Meanwhile, place the new potatoes in a steamer with the mint sprigs on top and cook for 15–20 minutes, until tender.

Heat a griddle pan until smoking hot. Add the lamb chops and courgette slices and cook for 2–3 minutes on each side, until the lamb is cooked to your liking and the courgettes are tender and nicely marked. Add the lemon wedges to the griddle for a minute or two, until nicely charred.

Arrange the lamb chops on warmed plates with the courgettes and lemon wedges. Add the steamed new potatoes and a dollop of the goat's curd or soft goat's cheese. Give a good grinding of black pepper to each one to serve.

SPRING LAMBS' LIVER ESCALOPES WITH SAGE AND SOFT POLENTA

SERVES 4

1 tbsp olive oil

40g (1½oz) butter

450g (1lb) spring lambs' liver, very thinly sliced into escalopes

4 slices prosciutto

12 fresh sage leaves

SOFT POLENTA:

500ml (18fl oz) chicken stock

500ml (18fl oz) milk

175g (6oz) instant polenta

75g (3oz) freshly grated Parmesan

4 heaped tbsp mascarpone cheese

sea salt and freshly ground black pepper

Everyone I know gets excited about spring lamb, but what about the liver? It never gets a look in. Traditionally liver has a bad rep in this country, as it is often served overcooked and thickly sliced. However, this dish has its origins in Italy, where spring lamb is highly anticipated and well worth the wait. Try it – you may be surprised.

To make the soft polenta, place the stock and milk in a pan over a high heat and bring to the boil. Whisk in the polenta and cook, stirring until smooth. Season to taste and stir in the Parmesan. Cover and keep warm until needed.

Heat a large non-stick frying pan over a high heat. Add half of the olive oil and a knob of the butter to the pan and then add half of the lambs' liver escalopes. Season to taste and cook briefly on each side until lightly browned but still pink in the middle. Transfer to a warmed plate and keep warm. Use the remaining oil and another knob of the butter to cook the rest of the lambs' liver escalopes, then transfer to the warmed plate as before.

Add the prosciutto to the heated pan with the sage leaves and quickly sear until crisp. Transfer to a plate lined with kitchen paper until needed. Add the rest of the butter to the pan and swirl it around to pick up all of the juices.

Place a dollop of the soft polenta into the middle of each warmed plate and swirl in a spoonful of the mascarpone cheese. Arrange the lambs' liver escalopes on top and scatter over the prosciutto and sage. Finally, drizzle with the pan juices to serve.

SEARED LAMB LOIN WITH BLACK OLIVE COUSCOUS AND YOGHURT SAUCE

SERVES 4

This recipe would also be great done on the barbecue. It uses Israeli couscous, which is also known as ptitim or Jerusalem couscous. It is actually an Israeli pasta shaped like rice or little balls. I like to eat it hot or cold and it has the added advantage of retaining its shape and texture even when reheated, as it does not clump together.

Preheat the oven to 200°C (400°F/gas mark 6). Put a large pan of water on a high heat and bring to the boil. Add the olive oil and a good amount of salt (2 tablespoons to 1.5 litres). Add the Israeli couscous and simmer for about 8 minutes or according to the packet instructions, until al dente. Drain and set aside.

Meanwhile, heat a heavy-based oven proof frying pan over a medium-high heat. Brush the lamb all over with the rapeseed oil and season to taste. Add the lamb loins to the pan and cook for 4–5 minutes, turning regularly, then transfer to the oven and cook for another 3 minutes, until medium-rare. Leave them in a little longer if you prefer your meat more well done. Transfer the lamb to a carving board and cover loosely with foil. Set aside for 5 minutes to rest.

Wipe out the frying pan and toast the almonds until lightly golden. Slice or halve the olives. Add the drained couscous to the pan, then fold in the almonds, olives and parsley and season to taste.

To make the yoghurt sauce, mix the yoghurt in a bowl with the spring onions, mint, dill, lemon juice and olive oil. Slowly whisk in enough water to make a smooth sauce. Season to taste.

Arrange the couscous to one side of warmed plates and then add a pool of the yoghurt sauce to each one. Carve the lamb into slices on the diagonal and arrange on top of the sauce to serve.

1 tbsp olive oil

300g (11oz) Israeli couscous

2 x 300g (11oz) boneless lamb loins, well trimmed

1 tbsp rapeseed oil

50g (2oz) blanched almonds, cut into slivers

100g (4oz) stoneless black olives

3 tbsp roughly chopped fresh flat-leaf parsley

YOGHURT SAUCE:

200g (7oz) thick Greek yoghurt

4 spring onions, finely minced

2 tbsp chopped fresh mint

2 tbsp chopped fresh dill

squeeze of lemon juice

dash of olive oil

sea salt and freshly ground black pepper

SICHUAN PEPPERED LAMB WITH SPICED REDCURRANT COMPOTE

SERVES 4

2 tbsp Sichuan peppercorns

2 tbsp black peppercorns

4 x 150g (5oz) lamb steaks, well trimmed

sunflower oil

knob of butter

fresh mint sprigs, to garnish

steamed new potatoes, to serve

SPICED REDCURRANT COMPOTE:

75g (3oz) caster sugar

1 cinnamon stick, crushed into tiny pieces, or 1 tsp ground cinnamon

pinch of dried chilli flakes

200g (7oz) redcurrants, removed from their stalks

good splash of ruby red port

The best way to remove redcurrants from their stems is to use a fork – simply hold the end of the stem and push through the prongs, dragging the fork down the stem. Not only does it save time, but it also doesn't damage the delicate fruit. I like the pieces of cinnamon in with the spiced redcurrants, but if this doesn't appeal, just use ground cinnamon.

To make the compote, place the sugar in a small heavy-based pan with 2 tablespoons of water. Cook over a gentle heat for a couple of minutes, stirring until the sugar has completely dissolved. Increase the heat to bring it to the boil and add the cinnamon and chilli, then boil fast for 1 minute. Add the redcurrants and the port. Reduce to a gentle simmer and cook for 4–5 minutes, until the berries are starting to soften but are still holding their shape. Remove from the heat and allow to stand for a few minutes so that the flavours can combine.

Meanwhile, using a pestle and mortar, grind down the peppercorns – you don't need a fine powder; a bit of texture is good. Rub each of the steaks with a little oil to help the peppercorns to stick, then press the peppercorn mixture onto each steak, making sure they are evenly coated.

Heat 1 tablespoon of oil in a large non-stick frying pan over a medium-high heat. Add the butter and when it is starting to foam, add the lamb steaks and cook for 2 minutes, then turn, reduce the heat slightly and cook for another 2–3 minutes for rare. If you prefer your steaks medium, increase the cooking time by 1 minute for each side. For well done, increase by 2 minutes for each side.

Transfer the lamb steaks to warmed serving plates and season with salt to taste. Leave to rest for a few minutes, then add a good dollop of the spiced redcurrant compote to each plate. Garnish with the mint sprigs and serve with some steamed new potatoes.

SPICED LAMB KEBABS ON FLATBREAD WITH ROASTED RED PEPPER HUMMUS

SERVES 4

500g (1lb 2oz) lean minced lamb

1 small onion, finely chopped

2 tsp chopped fresh oregano

1 tsp ground cumin

1 tsp hot paprika

½ tsp ground coriander

4 flatbreads or chapattis
(page 240)

lightly dressed mixed leaf salad,
to serve

lemon wedges, to garnish

ROASTED RED PEPPER
HUMMUS:

400g (14oz) can chickpeas,
drained and rinsed

1 roasted red pepper
(from a jar or a can)

1 mild red chilli, seeded and
chopped

2 garlic cloves, crushed

juice of 1 lemon

good pinch of ground cumin

100ml (3½fl oz) tahini
(sesame seed paste)

2 tbsp extra virgin olive oil

sea salt and freshly ground
black pepper

These kebabs are an excellent dish to serve to the whole family or a gang of hungry teenagers. As everything gets cooked under the grill there's the added bonus of very little washing up to do afterwards.

Preheat the grill to medium. Soak 20cm (8in) bamboo skewers in water.

Mix together the lamb with the onion, oregano, cumin, paprika and coriander. Season to taste and mix well to combine. Divide into 24 portions and then shape each piece into a cylinder that is 6cm (2½in) long. Thread 3 cylinders onto the bamboo skewers, reshaping as necessary. Arrange the lamb kebabs on a grill rack and cook for 10 minutes, turning occasionally, until well browned, cooked through and firm to the touch. Arrange on a wooden platter.

To make the hummus, place the chickpeas, red pepper, chilli, garlic, lemon juice, cumin and tahini in a food processor with 4 tablespoons of water. Whizz to a creamy purée and season to taste. Turn out into a wide-rimmed bowl and smooth with the back of a spoon. Drizzle with the extra virgin olive oil and some freshly ground black pepper.

To serve, warm the flatbreads or chapattis under the grill, turning once. Add the flatbreads to the wooden platter and put on the centre of the table with the bowl of roasted red pepper hummus, the mixed leaf salad and lemon wedges to garnish.

PORK

STICKY BACON CHOPS WITH ROOT VEGETABLE RÖSTI

SERVES 4

RÖSTI:

1 medium potato, peeled

1 medium carrot, peeled

1 small parsnip, peeled

75g (3oz) piece of turnip, peeled

2 tbsp snipped fresh chives

1 tbsp chopped fresh flat-leaf parsley

2 tbsp olive oil, plus extra if necessary

STICKY BACON CHOPS:

2 tsp olive oil

1 tbsp finely shredded orange rind

1 tsp fresh thyme leaves

4 thick-cut bacon chops

4 tbsp fresh orange juice

1 tbsp light muscovado sugar

sea salt and freshly ground black pepper

Have you ever seen bacon chops in the supermarket and wondered what to do with them? Well here is a recipe that all the family will enjoy. I'm serving them with crispy rösti, which cleverly disguises lots of nutritious root vegetables.

Preheat the oven to 200°C (400°F/gas mark 6).

To make the rösti, julienne the potato, carrot, parsnip and turnip on a mandolin or in a food processor. Put into a clean tea towel and squeeze out all of the excess water and starch. Place in a bowl and stir in the chives and parsley. Season to taste and mix well to combine.

Heat a large non-stick frying pan over a medium heat. Add the 2 tablespoons of olive oil to the pan and fry 8 heaped tablespoons of the vegetable mixture for 4–5 minutes on each side, until crisp and golden. Transfer to a non-stick baking sheet and cook for another 3–4 minutes in the oven, until completely cooked through.

Meanwhile, prepare the bacon chops. Heat another non-stick frying pan over a high heat. Add the oil, orange rind and thyme and cook for 2–3 minutes, until crisp. Remove from the pan and set to one side. Add the bacon chops and season with pepper, then cook for 2–3 minutes on each side, until lightly golden. Transfer to a plate.

Add the orange juice and sugar to the frying pan and cook until reduced. Return the bacon chops and crispy orange rind mixture to the pan and cook the bacon chops for another minute on each side, until heated through.

Arrange the bacon chops on warmed plates with the crispy vegetable rösti and spoon over the pan juices to serve.

MAPLE-GLAZED PORK CHOPS WITH PEAR AND ROCKET SALAD

SERVES 4

4 x 200g (7oz) pork cutlets, well trimmed

2 tbsp rapeseed oil

225ml (8fl oz) cider vinegar

8 tbsp maple syrup

1 tsp dried chilli flakes

2 long pieces of pared lemon rind

12 fresh sage leaves

2 small ripe pears

50g (2oz) wild rocket

olive oil, for drizzling

25g (1oz) Parmesan, pared into shavings

sea salt and freshly ground black pepper

This is a fantastic recipe that keeps the pork cutlets lovely and moist. It would also work with skinless, boneless chicken breasts. If you don't fancy using pear, try a nice dessert apple instead.

Heat a frying pan over a high heat. Rub the pork cutlets all over with the rapeseed oil and season to taste. Add to the pan and cook over a high heat for 2–3 minutes on each side, until well browned. Transfer to a plate.

Add the vinegar to the pan you've just cooked the pork in along with the maple syrup, chilli, lemon and sage. Bring to the boil and allow to boil for 5–6 minutes, until thickened slightly and syrupy. Return the pork cutlets to the pan and cook for 3–4 minutes on each side, or until the pork is cooked to your liking.

Meanwhile, cut the pears into quarters and remove the core, then arrange 2 pieces on each plate and scatter the rocket on top. Drizzle over the olive oil and sprinkle with the Parmesan shavings. Add a pork cutlet to each plate and spoon over some of the maple glaze to serve.

PORK MEATBALLS WITH CORIANDER AND COCONUT

SERVES 4

450g (1lb) lean minced pork

1 onion, very finely chopped

1 egg, lightly beaten

50g (2oz) fresh white breadcrumbs

1 red chilli, seeded and finely chopped

1 tsp garam masala

5cm (2in) piece root ginger, peeled and finely chopped

4 tbsp chopped fresh coriander

1 tbsp olive oil

2 tbsp mild curry paste

200g (7oz) canned or fresh tomatoes, chopped

250ml (9fl oz) carton coconut cream

1 tbsp lemon juice

steamed fragrant Thai jasmine rice, to serve

25g (1oz) toasted flaked almonds

lemon wedges, to garnish

sea salt and freshly ground black pepper

This is a fantastic recipe that my good friends at Bord Bia regularly demonstrate. It always goes down a treat with the crowd, so I thought it would be a great one to share with you. I've just slightly reduced the size of the meatballs so that they cook a little quicker in the oven.

Preheat the oven to 220°C (425°F/gas mark 7).

Place the minced pork in a bowl with the onion, egg, breadcrumbs, chilli, garam masala, half of the ginger and 2 tablespoons of the coriander. Season to taste and mix well to combine, then shape into 12 small balls approximately 2.5cm (1in) in diameter. Put the meatballs in a large roasting tin, drizzle over the olive oil and toss gently. Place in the oven for 10 minutes, until lightly golden.

While the meatballs are cooking, make the sauce. Heat a frying pan over a medium heat and add the curry paste and the remaining ginger. Cook for 1 minute, stirring constantly, then add the tomatoes and continue to cook for 2–3 minutes. Add the coconut cream and bring to the boil, then reduce the heat and simmer for 5 minutes.

Pour the sauce over the meatballs and quickly mix well to combine. Return to the oven for another 10 minutes, until the meatballs are cooked through and the sauce has reduced and thickened slightly.

Just before serving, stir in the lemon juice and arrange on plates with the rice. Scatter over the rest of the coriander and the almonds. Garnish with the lemon wedges to serve.

STIR-FRIED GINGER PORK WITH AROMATIC GREEN VEGETABLES

SERVES 4

This is a great way to prepare green vegetables. Stir-frying keeps their crunch while the hot sauce gives them a rich, almost nutty flavour. Choose one or a selection of the wide range of greens now readily available, such as tender stem broccoli, sugar snap peas, French beans, mangetout, spinach, Swiss chard, Chinese pak choy or choi sum, or even finely shredded cabbage works well.

Place 1 tablespoon of the sherry or rice wine and 1 tablespoon of the soy sauce in a shallow non-metallic dish and add the cornflour and sesame oil. Stir in the pork and set aside for 5 minutes.

Heat a wok until smoking hot. Add 1 tablespoon of the sunflower oil and swirl it up the sides of the wok. Tip in the pork and stir-fry for 3–4 minutes, until sealed and lightly golden. Transfer to a plate.

Meanwhile, place the remaining tablespoon of sherry and soy sauce in a small pan with the stock, then bring to a simmer.

Add the remaining tablespoon of sunflower oil to the wok. Add the ginger and stir-fry for 10 seconds. Tip in the mixed prepared greens and continue to stir-fry for 2–3 minutes, until heated through and any leaves are just beginning to wilt, splashing over a little water occasionally to help the greens cook.

Return the pork to the wok, then stir in the hot stock mixture. Cook for a minute or so until bubbling, stirring all the time. Spoon the steamed rice into warmed large Oriental-style bowls and spoon the ginger pork and greens on top. Scatter over the spring onions and chilli to serve.

2 tbsp dry sherry or rice wine

2 tbsp dark soy sauce

2 tsp cornflour

1 tsp sesame oil

450g (1lb) pork stir-fry strips

2 tbsp sunflower oil

120ml (4fl oz) chicken stock

5cm (2in) piece root ginger, peeled and finely grated

275g (10oz) mixed prepared greens (see intro)

2 spring onions, finely chopped

1 long red chilli, cut into thin rings

steamed fragrant Thai jasmine rice, to serve

GRILLED PORK SAUSAGES WITH SMOKED BAKED BEANS

SERVES 4

4 tbsp olive oil

1 large onion, finely chopped

2 celery sticks, finely chopped

2 garlic cloves, finely chopped

1 red chilli, seeded and finely chopped

1 tbsp chopped fresh sage

1 tsp smoked paprika

400g (14oz) can chopped tomatoes

2 tbsp tomato purée

2 x 400g (14oz) cans haricot beans, drained and rinsed

225g (8oz) Gubbeen cheese, cut into small dice

8 large hickory pork sausages (preferably McGettigan's)

1 tbsp chopped fresh flat-leaf parsley

sea salt and freshly ground black pepper

crusty bread, to serve

This is not a cassoulet in the true sense of the word, but the end result tastes nearly as good with very little effort. McGettigan Butchers in Donegal town are renowned for their award-winning sausages and were crowned European champions for their hickory and maple sausages, which are perfect in this cassoulet. For those of us in the rest of the country though, choose the sausages from the wide selection of good-quality sausages that are now widely available in major supermarkets and good butchers.

Preheat the oven to 180°C (350°F/gas mark 4) and preheat the grill to medium.

Heat the oil in an ovenproof frying pan or dish over a medium heat. Tip in the onion, celery, garlic, chilli and sage and sauté for about 5 minutes, until softened, stirring occasionally.

Stir the smoked paprika into the onion mixture and then add the tomatoes and the tomato purée. Bring to a simmer, then cook for another 5 minutes, until the sauce is slightly reduced and thickened, stirring occasionally. Season to taste. Stir in the haricot beans and sprinkle the Gubbeen cheese on top. Roast in the oven for 15 minutes, until the smoked baked beans are bubbling.

Meanwhile, arrange the hickory sausages on the grill rack and cook under a medium heat for about 5 minutes on each side, until cooked through and golden brown.

Scatter the parsley over the smoked baked beans and arrange the cooked sausages on top. Serve straight to the table with a bowl of crusty bread so that everyone can help themselves.

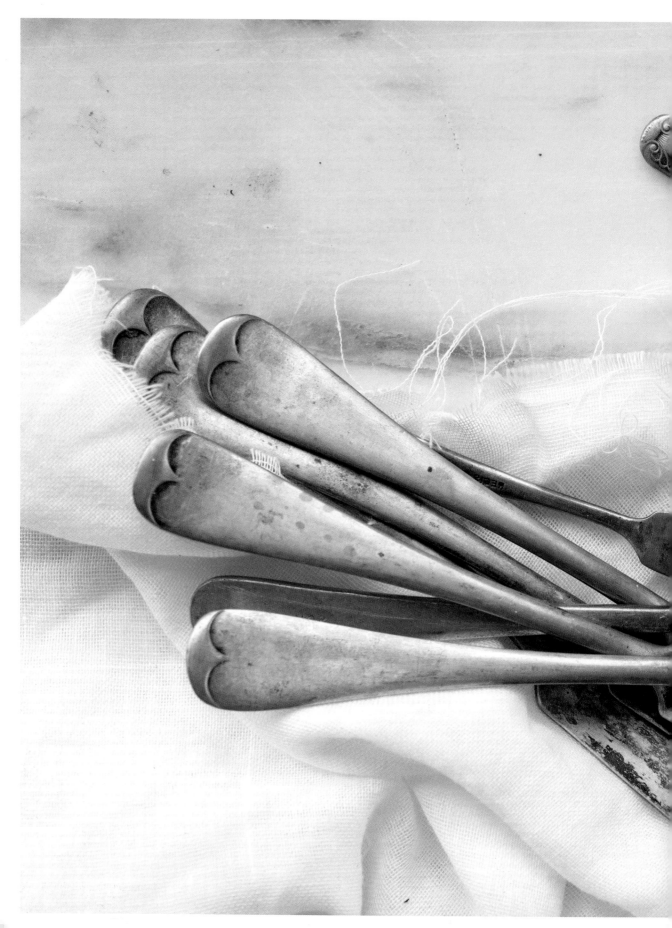

FISH

MACKEREL WITH SHERRY VINAIGRETTE AND NEW POTATO SALAD

SERVES 4

2 tbsp olive oil

4 mackerel fillets, skin on and pin bones removed

wild rocket leaves, to serve

SHERRY VINAIGRETTE:

4 tbsp extra virgin olive oil

2 tbsp sherry vinegar

1 tsp golden syrup

1 tsp wholegrain mustard

pinch of light muscovado sugar

NEW POTATO SALAD:

900g (2lb) waxy new potatoes (preferably small), scraped or scrubbed

2 tbsp light olive oil

2 tsp white wine vinegar

4 tbsp mayonnaise

2 tbsp crème fraîche

1 bunch spring onions, trimmed and thinly sliced

2 tbsp chopped fresh dill

2 tbsp chopped fresh flat-leaf parsley

sea salt and freshly ground black pepper

Mackerel is a great value fish. We are fortunate in being only half an hour from Bundoran, so it is available freshly caught and ready to go. Mackerel is an oil-rich fish that is naturally low in saturated fat, full of vitamins and minerals, and an excellent source of essential omega-3 fats. The body cannot make omega-3 fats, so to ensure you get a regular supply, you should eat oily fish such as mackerel, salmon or trout at least once a week.

First make the potato salad. If necessary, cut the potatoes into 2.5cm (1in) chunks. Place in a pan of salted water, bring to the boil and cook for 12–15 minutes, until tender. Meanwhile, whisk together the olive oil and white wine vinegar in a large bowl and season to taste. Drain the potatoes well, toss into this dressing and leave to cool completely.

Meanwhile, make the sherry vinaigrette for the mackerel. Place the olive oil in a screw-top jar with the sherry vinegar, golden syrup, mustard and sugar. Season to taste and shake vigorously until emulsified. Set aside until needed.

To cook the mackerel, heat the olive oil in a non-stick frying pan over a medium-high heat. Season the mackerel fillets and make small incisions in the skin to prevent them from curling up. Add to the pan and cook for 5–7 minutes, turning once, until the skin is crisp and the mackerel is cooked through.

To finish the potato salad, stir the mayonnaise and crème fraîche together in a small bowl, then stir into the potatoes along with the spring onions, dill and parsley and season to taste.

To serve, place the mackerel fillets on warmed serving plates. Drizzle the sherry vinaigrette around the plate, garnish with rocket leaves and serve with new potato salad.

ROASTED HAKE WITH CHERRY TOMATOES, BASIL AND MOZZARELLA

SERVES 4

4 x 175g (6oz) hake fillets, skin on and pin bones removed

12 cherry tomatoes, thinly sliced

small handful of fresh basil leaves, roughly torn

120g (4½oz) ball of buffalo mozzarella, sliced

2 tbsp basil pesto (shop-bought or homemade)

sea salt and freshly ground black pepper

lightly dressed green salad, to serve

buttered baby boiled potatoes tossed in snipped fresh chives, to serve

Hake has a lovely soft texture and slight sweetness when it is very fresh. It is highly regarded by chefs as it offers great value for money. Ask your fishmonger for the hake fillets from the centre cut so that they are nice and chunky. This will also help them cook more evenly.

Preheat the oven to 200°C (400°F/gas mark 6).

Place the hake on a baking sheet, skin side down, and season the flesh. Arrange the tomato slices on top and tuck in the basil leaves. Cover with the mozzarella and drizzle over the pesto.

Place the hake in the oven and bake for 15–20 minutes, until the hake is cooked through and the mozzarella is bubbling and lightly golden. Transfer the hake with cherry tomatoes, basil and mozzarella to warmed plates and have bowls of green salad and buttered baby boiled potatoes to hand around separately.

SEA BASS WITH CHORIZO CASSOULET

SERVES 4

This recipe has a real Spanish flavour and is very easy to prepare. This way of cooking fish retains the goodness and keeps the fish moist. Fish has become expensive, but sea bass has remained good value, as it is nearly all farmed these days. Line-caught sea bass is now a very rare and highly prized fish.

Preheat the oven to 200°C (400°F/gas mark 6).

Heat 1 tablespoon of the rapeseed oil in a heavy-based pan over a medium-high heat. Add the chorizo and sauté for 2–3 minutes, until sizzling. Remove the chorizo and drain on kitchen paper.

To prepare the sea bass, score the skin in thin parallel lines using a very sharp knife and season the flesh side lightly, then cut each fillet in half on the diagonal. Heat a non-stick frying pan over a medium heat and add the oil and butter. Once the butter stops sizzling, add the sea bass, skin side down, and cook gently for 4–5 minutes to get the skin crispy, then carefully turn over and cook for 2–3 minutes to brown lightly. Sea bass is best served slightly pink and still quite moist.

Meanwhile, pour the stock into a pan and add the cooked chorizo and the mixed beans. Bring to the boil, then reduce the heat and simmer for a few minutes, until warmed through. Season to taste, then whisk in the butter and stir in the parsley and chives.

Spoon some chorizo cassoulet in the centre of each warmed plate and arrange the sea bass alongside, skin side up. Garnish with baby salad leaves and serve.

4 x 150g (5oz) sea bass fillets, pin bones removed and scaled

1 tbsp rapeseed oil

1 tsp softened butter

CHORIZO CASSOULET:

1 tbsp rapeseed oil

100g (4oz) raw chorizo, skinned and diced

150ml (¼ pint) vegetable stock

400g (14oz) can mixed beans, drained and rinsed (such as haricot, cannellini, borlotti and black-eyed beans)

1 tbsp softened butter

2 tsp roughly chopped fresh flat-leaf parsley

1 tsp snipped fresh chives

baby salad leaves, to garnish

sea salt and freshly ground black pepper

SALMON BURGERS WITH ROASTED RED PEPPER SALSA

SERVES 4

550g (1¼lb) salmon fillet, skinned and boned (well chilled)

2 spring onions, thinly sliced

1 heaped tbsp Dijon mustard or wasabi paste

2 tsp sesame seeds

1 tbsp seasoned flour

2 tbsp olive oil

4 slices sourdough bread

4 Little Gem lettuce leaves

handful of fresh coriander sprigs

lime wedges, to serve

ROASTED RED PEPPER SALSA:

2 roasted red peppers, finely diced (from a jar is fine)

2 plum tomatoes, seeded and finely chopped

finely grated rind of 1 lemon

2 tbsp sweet chilli sauce

1 tbsp rapeseed oil

1 tbsp chopped fresh coriander

1 tbsp shredded fresh basil

sea salt and freshly ground black pepper

These burgers need nothing to bind the salmon except the mustard or wasabi paste (which is a Japanese horseradish available in tubes from the Asian section of the supermarket) and would work well with any firm-fleshed fish, such as tuna or hake. Ask the fish counter to ensure that all the skin and bones have been removed.

Using a large sharp knife, cut away any brown bits from the salmon fillet, then finely chop. Place in a bowl, then stir in the spring onions, mustard and sesame seeds. Season to taste. Divide into 4 portions, then using slightly wetted hands, shape into patties. Dust the patties in the flour, shaking off any excess. Place in the fridge for 10 minutes to firm up.

Meanwhile, make the roasted red pepper salsa. Place the red peppers in a bowl and stir in the tomatoes, lemon rind, sweet chilli sauce, oil and herbs. Season to taste and set aside at room temperature to allow the flavours to develop.

Heat a large non-stick frying pan over a medium heat. Add the olive oil to the frying pan and then add the salmon burgers. Cook for 3–4 minutes on each side, until lightly golden but still slightly pink in the centre. Be careful not to overcook them or they will quickly become dry. Set aside.

Meanwhile, heat a griddle pan until smoking hot. Add the slices of sourdough bread and chargrill for 1–2 minutes on each side, until nicely marked. Arrange on warmed plates and top with Little Gem lettuce leaves and the burgers. Spoon over the roasted red pepper salsa, then scatter over the coriander sprigs and serve with lime wedges.

BAKED FISH FILLETS WITH HORSERADISH CRUST AND LEMON CREAM SAUCE

SERVES 4

50g (2oz) plain flour

4 x 175g (6oz) firm fish fillets, such as salmon, hake, cod or haddock, skinned and boned

2 tbsp creamed horseradish (from a jar)

1 egg yolk

100g (4oz) coarse breadcrumbs

1 tbsp chopped fresh flat-leaf parsley

LEMON CREAM SAUCE:

225ml (8fl oz) cream

1 tsp Dijon mustard

1 tsp prepared English mustard

1 tsp creamed horseradish (from a jar)

finely grated rind and juice of ½ lemon

1 tbsp snipped fresh chives

WILTED SPINACH:

75g (3oz) butter

450g (1lb) spinach, tough stalks removed

pinch of sugar

sea salt and freshly ground black pepper

I was first shown how to cook this dish by Paul Rankin at Roscoff in Belfast, which has now sadly closed. I was only a wee young chap and it was my first impression of a Michelin star kitchen, which I'll never forget. This is an extremely easy dish to master and perfect to serve on a special occasion if you want to get ahead, as the fish can be prepped and set aside in the fridge until it's ready to go into the oven.

Preheat the oven to 200°C (400°F/gas mark 6). Line a sturdy baking sheet with parchment paper.

Season the flour in a shallow bowl and use to lightly dust the fish fillets. To make the crust, mix together the horseradish and egg yolk, then spread on top of each fish fillet, making sure each one is well coated right to the edges. Mix together the breadcrumbs and parsley and then press them on each coated piece of fish. Shape the crust by pressing on this mixture gently but firmly with your hands. Arrange the crusted fish fillets on the lined baking sheet. Place in the oven for 15–20 minutes, until the fish fillets are just cooked through and tender and the crusts are nice and crisp.

Meanwhile, make the lemon cream sauce. Place the cream in a small pan and bring to the boil, then reduce the heat and allow to simmer for 12 minutes, until well reduced and thickened. Remove from the heat and whisk in the mustards, horseradish, the lemon rind and juice and season to taste. Stir in the chives and keep warm over a low heat.

To prepare the wilted spinach, heat a large pan over a medium heat and add the butter. Once it has stopped foaming, quickly sauté the spinach with a pinch of sugar until soft and wilted. Season to taste and drain well on kitchen paper to remove the excess moisture.

To serve, divide the spinach among warmed plates. Place a piece of fish on top and drizzle around the lemon cream sauce.

EGGS

EGGS ON TOAST

SERVES 4

4 large slices sourdough bread

50g (2oz) butter, at room temperature

4 large eggs

8 slices Parma ham

sea salt and freshly ground black pepper

lightly dressed rocket and Parmesan salad, to serve

This is a very trendy version of eggs on toast that has been brought bang up to date with the ingredients used. It's the kind of recipe that you could pick everything up at a farmers' market on the weekend and have for brunch or a light supper, depending on how you want to spend your day. It would also be delicious with crispy streaky bacon and some wilted spinach.

Heat a large non-stick frying pan over a low heat. Using a 5cm (2in) straight-sided cutter, stamp out a hole in the middle of each slice of bread (these can be discarded or eaten, depending on how hungry you are!). Butter both sides of each slice of bread.

Add a piece of buttered bread to the heated frying pan and cook for about 3 minutes, until golden, then turn over and crack an egg into the hole of the bread. Cook for another 2–3 minutes or until the eggs are cooked to your liking. Place on a warm plate and either serve immediately or keep warm while you cook the remainder.

Just before serving, arrange the Parma ham to the side of the eggs on toast and add a small pile of the rocket and Parmesan salad to each one. Finish with a grinding of black pepper and a pinch of salt on the yolk of the egg.

CRISPY HEN EGGS WITH STEAK TARTARE

SERVES 4

This recipe is from my good pal Stephen Gibson, who co-owns Pichet Restaurant in Dublin, a modern take on the classic bistro. This has been their signature dish since they opened, although Stephen is constantly changing it depending on the season – this is his current favourite version and it really is sensational.

To make the tarragon mayonnaise, break the egg into a food processor and add the garlic, vinegar, mustard, salt, sugar and about 4 tablespoons of the oil. Secure the lid and whizz for 10 seconds. Leave to stand for a couple of seconds, then turn it on again and pour the remaining oil through a feeder tube in a thin, steady stream. This should take 25–30 seconds. Switch off the machine, take off the lid, scrape down the sides and add the tarragon leaves. Whizz again for 2–3 seconds and season to taste. Transfer to a squeezy bottle and chill until needed.

To prepare the dressing for the steak tartare, place the tomato ketchup in a bowl and add the mustard, capers, gherkins, shallots, paprika and Tabasco and season to taste. Set aside until needed.

To poach the eggs, bring a large pan of water to a gentle simmer and add the vinegar. Break in 4 of the eggs, one at a time, where the water is bubbling and poach for 3 minutes, until just cooked through. Remove with a slotted spoon and refresh in cold water to prevent them from cooking any further. Pat dry with kitchen paper.

TARRAGON MAYONNAISE:

1 egg, at room temperature

1 small garlic clove, crushed

1 tsp white wine vinegar

1 tsp Dijon mustard

½ tsp salt

pinch of caster sugar

200ml (7fl oz) sunflower oil

good handful of fresh tarragon leaves

CRISPY HEN EGGS:

2 tsp white wine vinegar

6 eggs, at room temperature (preferably organic)

sunflower oil, for deep-frying

25g (1oz) plain flour

100g (4oz) panko breadcrumbs (dried and toasted)

STEAK TARTARE:

100g (4oz) tomato ketchup

2 heaped tbsp Dijon mustard

2 heaped tbsp finely
chopped capers

2 heaped tbsp finely
chopped gherkins

2 heaped tbsp finely diced shallots

¼ tsp smoked paprika

dash of Tabasco

175g (6oz) beef fillet, well
trimmed and finely diced

baby salad leaves, to serve

sea salt and freshly ground
black pepper

Heat the sunflower oil in a deep-fat fryer or straight-sided pan to 180°C (350°F). Place the flour on a flat plate and season lightly, then crack the remaining 2 eggs into a shallow dish and beat lightly. Put the breadcrumbs into a separate shallow dish. Coat the poached eggs in the seasoned flour and then dip in the beaten egg, then cover in the breadcrumbs. Deep-fry the coated eggs for 2–3 minutes, until crisp and golden brown. Drain well on kitchen paper.

Meanwhile, fold the fillet steak into the prepared tartare dressing and spoon into a 6cm (2½in) cooking ring on each plate. Add a good dollop of the tarragon mayonnaise to each one. Arrange the baby salad leaves around it and top each one with a crispy hen egg. Serve at once.

EGG AND SPINACH BRUNCH

SERVES 4

2 tbsp olive oil

1 large red onion, thinly sliced

675g (1½lb) leftover cooked potatoes, peeled and roughly chopped

25g (1oz) butter

½ tsp fresh soft thyme leaves

200g (7oz) frozen leaf spinach

4 eggs

25g (1oz) strong Cheddar cheese, finely grated

sea salt and freshly ground black pepper

crispy French baguette, to serve

This brunch dish depends on you having some leftover cooked potatoes in the fridge. It's a delicious dish that can go straight on the table and would be lovely on its own or with some grilled streaky bacon or even gutsy flavoured sausages. You decide.

Preheat the oven to 200°C (400°F/gas mark 6).

Heat the oil in a large ovenproof frying pan. Add the onions and cook over a high heat for a couple of minutes, until softened. Tip in the potatoes and toss until evenly coated, then continue to cook over a high heat for another 3–4 minutes, until the potatoes are starting to catch colour. Add the butter and thyme and toss until evenly coated, then season to taste and put in the oven for 10 minutes.

Meanwhile, place the spinach in a small pan and cook until soft, according to the packet instructions. Remove the potato and onion mixture from the oven and quickly add small mounds of spinach. Make 4 indentations for the eggs and break them in. Sprinkle the Cheddar cheese on top and return to the oven for 8–10 minutes, until the eggs are lightly set. Serve straight to the table with crispy French baguette.

SOUFFLÉ OMELETTE WITH SMOKED HADDOCK

SERVES 4

This is actually very similar to the classic omelette Arnold Bennett. Properly cooked, it is absolutely delicious and I've no doubt your guests will savour every mouthful. If you are really short of time, substitute smoked mackerel fillets and flake as for the recipe, which will save you having to poach the fish.

450ml (¾ pint) milk

450g (1lb) smoked haddock fillet, skinned and boned

75g (3oz) Gruyère cheese, grated

25g (1oz) freshly grated Parmesan cheese

75ml (3fl oz) cream

12 eggs

50g (2oz) butter

4 ripe tomatoes, sliced

sea salt and freshly ground white pepper

snipped fresh chives, to garnish

baby spinach salad, to serve

Pour the milk into a saucepan and bring to a gentle simmer. Add in the haddock and poach for about 3 minutes. Remove it from the pan and flake it, discarding any stray skin and bones. Mix the flaked haddock with the two cheeses, setting aside a handful of the cheese mix for grilling later. Season to taste.

Meanwhile, gently heat the cream in a small heavy-based pan until it has reduced by one-third.

To make each omelette, preheat the grill to hot. Whisk together 3 of the eggs and season to taste. Melt a little butter in an omelette pan. Pour the eggs into the hot pan and move gently about so that all the egg mixture comes in contact with the hot pan.

Divide the fish and cheese mixture into 4 portions. Place one portion on top of the omelette and let it warm through for a few minutes, until the underside of the omelette is golden brown.

Pour over a little of the reduced cream, add a layer of the sliced tomatoes and finish with a final sprinkling of the cheese mix. Place the omelette under the hot grill for 2 minutes. Slide the omelette onto a warmed plate and serve without folding. Scatter over the chives to garnish. Repeat with the remaining ingredients until you have made 4 omelettes. Serve at once with a separate dish of spinach salad.

BAKED EGGS WITH TOMATOES AND MATURE CHEDDAR CHEESE

SERVES 4

butter, for greasing

2 ripe vine tomatoes, peeled, seeded and finely chopped

4 large eggs

4 tbsp cream

25g (1oz) mature Cheddar cheese, finely grated

1 tsp snipped fresh chives

sea salt and freshly ground black pepper

griddled sourdough bread sliced into chunky fingers, to serve

Experiment with other flavour additions – a little chopped cooked ham or Parma ham, diced cooked mushrooms, a few herbs or some sliced artichoke heart can all go into the base before you crack in the egg. For a really extravagant addition, add a drop or two of white truffle oil over the cream.

Preheat the oven to 190°C (375°F/gas mark 5).

Butter 4 blini pans or ramekins and scatter the tomatoes in the bottom. Crack an egg into each blini pan and season with salt, then add 1 tablespoon of cream to each one and scatter the Cheddar on top.

Arrange the blini pans in a shallow roasting tin and pour in enough boiling water to come about halfway up the side of each pan. Place in the oven and bake for 15 minutes, until the eggs are set and the cheese is bubbling. Set each blini pan on a plate and scatter over the chives, then add the chunky bread fingers to serve.

VEGETARIAN

WILD MUSHROOM AND SPINACH GALETTE

SERVES 4

425g (15oz) packet frozen ready-rolled puff pastry, thawed

rocket, to garnish

MUSHROOM DUXELLES:

1 tbsp rapeseed oil

175g (6oz) mixed wild mushrooms, diced

1 large shallot, chopped

1 large garlic clove, crushed

2 tsp Madeira

2 tsp cream

2 tsp chopped fresh mixed herbs (such as chives, basil and flat-leaf parsley)

WILTED SPINACH:

75g (3oz) butter

350g (12oz) spinach, tough stalks removed

pinch of sugar

sea salt and freshly ground black pepper

A wonderful vegetarian tart that is full of flavour. Try to source an all-butter puff pastry if you can, or you could always make your own...

Preheat the oven to 200°C (400°F/gas mark 6). Line 2 baking sheets with parchment paper.

Unroll the 2 pieces of puff pastry and place on a lightly floured board. Cut out 4 x 15cm (6in) circles and place on the lined baking sheets. Mark a thin rim around the edge and then prick the inner circle of pastry to prevent it from puffing up, making a slight dip for the topping. Lay another sheet of parchment paper over the pastry circles and cover with a second baking sheet. This will prevent them from rising too much and makes them extra crispy and golden brown. Bake for about 15 minutes, until lightly golden, swapping the baking sheets around on the oven shelves halfway through so they cook evenly.

Meanwhile, to prepare the mushroom duxelles, heat the rapeseed oil in a large frying pan over a medium heat. Add the mushrooms, shallot and garlic and sauté for 1–2 minutes, until just tender. Add the Madeira, cream and herbs. Reduce for 2 minutes, then season to taste. Remove from the heat and leave to cool.

To make the wilted spinach, heat a large pan over a medium heat and add the butter. Once it has stopped foaming, quickly sauté the spinach with a pinch of sugar until soft and wilted. Season to taste and drain on kitchen paper to remove the excess moisture.

Divide the wilted spinach evenly among the cooked pastry cases, spreading it out to the rim using the back of a spoon. Spoon the mushroom duxelles on top and flash through the oven again for another 4–5 minutes, until heated through. Arrange on warmed plates and garnish with rocket to serve.

RICOTTA RAVIOLI WITH SWISS CHARD AND GARLIC RAPESEED OIL

SERVES 4

1 tbsp rapeseed oil

1 small red onion, finely diced

2 garlic cloves, finely chopped

4 Swiss or ruby chard leaves, tough stalks removed (if unavailable, use 100g (4oz) tender young spinach leaves)

200g (7oz) ricotta cheese

1 tbsp chopped fresh basil

24 wonton wrappers, thawed if frozen

a little plain flour, for dusting

a little egg wash, for brushing

garlic rapeseed oil, for drizzling

25g (1oz) wild rocket

25g (1oz) Parmesan, pared into shavings

4 tbsp toasted pine nuts

fresh rocket flowers, to garnish (optional)

sea salt and freshly ground black pepper

This ravioli is a clever way of looking like you have gone to the trouble of making your own pasta, but it uses wonton wrappers, which are available in Asian supermarkets. However, they do need to be made fresh and don't benefit from hanging around.

Heat the rapeseed oil in a pan and sauté the onion and garlic for about for 5 minutes, until softened but not coloured. Add the Swiss or ruby chard and cook for 2–3 minutes, until just wilted, stirring regularly. Remove from the heat and leave to cool completely.

Squeeze out any excess moisture from the Swiss chard mixture and then finely chop. Place in a bowl and stir in the ricotta cheese and basil. Season to taste and mix well to combine.

Place 12 wonton wrappers on a lightly floured work surface and spoon a heaped teaspoon of the Swiss chard mixture into the centre of each one. Brush the edges with egg wash and then carefully cover with the remaining wonton wrappers, pressing gently to shape into ravioli. You can use a small fluted cutter to shape each ravioli if you like and discard the leftover scraps of wonton pastry.

To cook the ravioli, bring a large pan of salted water to the boil. Add the ravioli and cook for about 2 minutes, until just cooked through and they are floating at the top of the pan. Drain well and arrange on warmed plates. Drizzle over the garlic rapeseed oil and scatter over the wild rocket, then sprinkle the Parmesan shavings and toasted pine nuts on top. Scatter over the rocket flowers, if using, and serve at once.

LINGUINE WITH PORCINI, ARTICHOKES AND PARMESAN CREAM

SERVES 4

25g (1oz) dried porcini mushrooms

2 tbsp olive oil

1 onion, diced

2 garlic cloves, crushed

1 tsp chopped fresh thyme

150ml (¼ pint) dry white wine

finely grated rind and juice
of 1 lemon

450g (1lb) linguine

200ml (7fl oz) cream

275g (10oz) jar artichoke hearts,
drained and halved

50g (2oz) freshly grated
Parmesan, plus extra shavings
to garnish

50g (2oz) wild rocket

1 tbsp chopped fresh
flat-leaf parsley

sea salt and freshly ground
black pepper

Although porcini mushrooms are expensive, just a small amount added to a dish will make an enormous difference to the flavour. They taste intensely savoury and concentrated in this creamy pasta dish.

Soak the porcini mushrooms in a bowl of just-boiled water for 10 minutes.

Meanwhile, heat the olive oil in a heavy-based pan over a medium heat. Tip in the onion and garlic and sauté for about 3 minutes, until softened but not coloured. Stir in the thyme, then pour in the wine and lemon juice and cook for 5 minutes, until slightly reduced, stirring occasionally.

Drain the soaked porcini mushrooms, reserving the liquid, and then finely chop. Add to the wine mixture with the reserved soaking liquid and simmer for 5–6 minutes, or until reduced by half.

Meanwhile, cook the linguine in a large pan of boiling salted water for 10–12 minutes, until al dente, or according to the packet instructions.

Stir the cream into the reduced porcini mixture and then fold in the artichoke hearts and Parmesan. Simmer very gently for 5–6 minutes, until slightly thickened and heated through. Stir in the rocket, parsley and lemon rind and cook for another 1–2 minutes, until the rocket is just wilted. Season to taste.

Drain the pasta and shake well to remove any excess water, then stir in the porcini and artichoke sauce and divide among warmed pasta bowls. Scatter over a little extra Parmesan to garnish and serve immediately.

MEDITERRANEAN VEGETABLE AND BOILÍE PIZZA TART

SERVES 4

A wonderful vegetarian tart that is really light and full of flavour. I like to serve this with a red pepper purée, which is simply a jar or can of roasted red peppers blended with some flavoured oil and seasoning.

Preheat the oven to 200°C (400°F/gas mark 6). Line a baking sheet with parchment paper.

Unroll the puff pastry and place on a clean work surface. Cut into quarters and place on the lined baking sheet. Prick the pastry all over many times to prevent it from puffing up. Lay another sheet of parchment paper over the pastry pieces and cover with a second baking sheet. This will prevent them from rising too much and make them extra crispy and golden brown. Bake for 15–18 minutes, until slightly puffed up and lightly golden, swapping the baking sheets around on the oven shelves halfway through to ensure they cook evenly.

Meanwhile, heat the rapeseed oil in a frying pan and sauté the courgette, red onion and aubergine on a medium heat for 8–10 minutes, until the vegetables are beginning to soften and catch colour. Season to taste and stir in the diced roasted peppers and 2 tablespoons of the basil pesto.

Divide the sautéed vegetables evenly among the pastry cases, spreading them out nearly to the rim using the back of a spoon. Arrange 6 Boilíe goat's cheese balls on top of each tart and drizzle over the remaining tablespoon of basil pesto. Return to the oven for 6–8 minutes, until the tarts have completely warmed through.

Arrange the pizza tarts on warmed plates and garnish with the fresh basil, toasted pine nuts and nasturtium flowers and leaves. Serve with a small pot of red pepper purée, if liked.

320g (11oz) packet frozen ready-rolled puff pastry, thawed

2 tbsp rapeseed oil

1 small courgette, cut into dice

1 small red onion, cut into dice

100g (4oz) aubergine, cut into dice

2 roasted red peppers, cut into dice (from a jar or can)

3 tbsp basil pesto (shop-bought or homemade)

24 Boilíe goat's cheese balls, drained (from jars)

sea salt and freshly ground black pepper

fresh baby basil leaves, to garnish

2 tbsp toasted pine nuts, to garnish

nasturtium flowers and leaves, to garnish

red pepper purée, to serve (optional – see intro)

SPICY POTATO AND CHICKPEA PATTIES

SERVES 4

sunflower oil, for frying

1 onion, finely chopped

2.5cm (1in) piece root ginger, peeled and grated

1 long green chilli, seeded and finely chopped

1 tsp garam masala

½ tsp ground cumin

½ tsp ground turmeric

450g (1lb) leftover cooked, peeled potatoes

400g (14oz) can chickpeas, rinsed and drained

2 tbsp desiccated coconut

2 tbsp plain flour, plus extra for dusting

juice of ½ lemon

sea salt and freshly ground black pepper

chapattis, to serve

cucumber raita, to serve

cherry tomato salad, to serve

This is a quick and easy vegetarian meal that uses up leftover cooked potatoes, whether they are mashed or whole. The end result is completely delicious. Serve them as a main course with some shop-bought chapattis, a cherry tomato salad and a refreshing cucumber raita. They would also make a great side dish or snack.

Heat 1 tablespoon of oil in a frying pan over a medium heat and fry the onion for a few minutes, until softened. Add the ginger and chilli and cook for 1 minute. Stir in the garam masala, cumin and turmeric and cook for another minute or so.

If the potatoes are already mashed, just put them into a large bowl. If they are whole, roughly chop them. Roughly chop the chickpeas and add to the potatoes. Remove the onion mixture from the heat and beat into the potato and chickpea mixture.

Add the coconut, flour, lemon juice and seasoning to the potato mixture and stir well to combine. Divide the mixture into 20 balls, lightly dust in a little more flour and then shape into small patties.

Wipe out the frying pan and heat with a couple of tablespoons of oil. Cook the patties in batches for 6–8 minutes, until crisp and lightly golden, turning once. Serve hot with the chapattis, cucumber raita and a cherry tomato salad.

TAKEAWAY
MY WAY

PUMPKIN PIZZA WITH CASHEL BLUE AND PICKLED RED ONION

MAKES 2 LARGE PIZZAS

3 tbsp olive oil, plus extra to drizzle

450g (1lb) pumpkin, peeled, seeded and diced

2 large ready-made artisan pizza bases (see intro)

225g (8oz) Cashel Blue cheese, broken into chunks

2 handfuls of wild rocket leaves

PICKLED RED ONION:

4 tbsp caster sugar

4 tbsp red wine vinegar

1 red onion, very thinly sliced (on a mandolin is best)

sea salt and freshly ground black pepper

These authentic pizzas are incredibly easy to make, as you only need to prepare the toppings. Pizza da Piero artisan pizza bases are now readily available in supermarkets and good delis. They are made in Ireland and make a fantastic pizza that will be better than anything you can order to be delivered.

Preheat the oven to 240°C (475°F/gas mark 9).

Heat the oil in a heavy-based frying pan over a medium-high heat. Sauté the pumpkin for 8–10 minutes, until it is cooked through but still holding its shape.

Meanwhile, make the pickled red onions. Put the sugar and vinegar in a small pan and bring to a simmer until the sugar has dissolved. Remove from the heat and add the red onion slices. Season to taste and set aside to allow the flavours to combine.

Put the pizza bases on 2 large baking sheets and arrange the sautéed pumpkin and Cashel Blue on top. Bake for about 5 minutes, until the base is crisp and the blue cheese has melted. Remove the pizza from the oven and add mounds of the sweet pickled red onion, draining it of any excess liquid. Scatter over the rocket, drizzle with a little olive oil and transfer to warmed platters to serve straight to the table.

VARIATION

If you prefer a more traditional pizza, sauté an onion until softened and then add a can of plum tomatoes and a pinch of sugar. Season to taste and mash to a pulp with a potato masher. Blitz to a purée with a hand blender and then spread as a tomato topping on the pizza bases. Top with chunks of raw chorizo and mozzarella and a sprinkling of pink peppercorns, or try slices of Milleens cheese with pieces of sun-dried tomatoes for a change.

FISH AND CHIPS

SERVES 4

There is probably nothing nicer than freshly cooked fish and chips, and this recipe is hard to beat. Once the fish is cooked it should only be kept warm for a minute or two while you finish cooking the chips so that the batter doesn't lose any of its crispness.

To make the chips, peel the potatoes and cut into strips no more than 1cm (½in) thick. Wash well in cold water to remove excess starch, then drain well. Transfer to a clean tea towel and shake until completely dry.

Heat the oil in a deep-fat fryer to 160°C (320°F). Place half of the chips in a wire basket and carefully lower into the oil. Cook until the chips are soft and flexible but not browned. Remove the chips and drain well on kitchen paper. Bring the oil up to 180°C (350°F) again and par-cook the remaining chips. Set aside until needed.

Meanwhile, make the fish goujons. Cut the whiting fillets into strips that are about 1cm (½in) wide and 10cm (4in) long and season generously. To make the batter, place the flour, cornflour, cider and a pinch of salt into a liquidiser and blend until smooth (or use a hand blender).

8 potatoes, such as Maris Piper

2 litres (3½ pints) sunflower or vegetable oil

900g (2lb) skinless whiting fillets, pin bones removed

50g (2oz) plain flour

lemon wedges, to serve

crushed peas, to serve

salt and malt vinegar, for seasoning

BATTER:

150g (5oz) plain flour

50g (2oz) cornflour

350ml (12fl oz) chilled dry cider (such as Stonewell)

Increase the heat of the oil to 185°C (365°F). Season the flour and place in a shallow dish. Dust the fish in the seasoned flour and then dip into the batter, gently shaking off any excess. Carefully lower into the hot oil. Deep-fry for 6–7 minutes, until the fish is cooked through and the batter is crisp and golden. Drain well on kitchen paper and keep warm in a low oven.

To finish cooking the chips, bring the oil temperature down to 175°C (345°F). Quickly cook half of the cooled chips for 1–2 minutes, until they are golden brown. Drain on kitchen paper and then cook the rest of chips in the same way.

Arrange the fish goujons and chips on plates with lemon wedges and the crushed peas. Season with salt and malt vinegar before serving.

SIZZLING BEEF WITH BLACK BEANS AND BROCCOLI

SERVES 4

If you don't want to use purple sprouting broccoli, try long-stemmed broccoli, or even asparagus would work well. All will give an excellent crunch to this dish, which is far superior to anything you would order from a takeaway.

Cut the beef into thin slices, then place in a bowl. Make the marinade with the soy sauce, rice wine, sesame oil and cornflour. Season to taste and mix well to combine. Set aside at room temperature for 5 minutes to allow the flavours to combine.

Meanwhile, trim down the broccoli and cut into 7.5cm (3in) pieces on the diagonal and set aside until needed.

Heat a wok or large frying pan until very hot. Add the oil and swirl it around until it's very hot and slightly smoking. Tip in the beef from the marinade and stir-fry for 2 minutes. Remove with a slotted spoon and drain in a colander.

Tip the onion into the wok with the garlic, black beans and ginger and stir-fry for 1 minute. Add the broccoli and stir-fry for another minute. Add the stock, rice wine and sugar and season to taste. Continue to stir-fry for 1–2 minutes, until the broccoli is slightly tender.

Quickly return the beef to the wok, add the oyster sauce and stir well to combine. Place on warmed plates with some steamed rice to serve.

450g (1lb) beef fillet

350g (12oz) purple sprouting broccoli

2 tbsp sunflower oil

1 onion, thinly sliced

4 garlic cloves, finely chopped

2 tbsp Chinese black beans, coarsely chopped

2 tsp finely chopped root ginger

3 tbsp chicken stock

1 tbsp Chinese rice wine

1 tsp sugar

2 tbsp oyster sauce

steamed rice, to serve

MARINADE:

2 tsp light soy sauce

2 tsp Chinese rice wine

2 tsp sesame oil

2 tsp cornflour

sea salt and freshly ground black pepper

CRISPY BUTTERMILK CHICKEN WITH CELERIAC SLAW

SERVES 4

2 x 200g (7oz) skinless chicken fillets

300ml (½ pint) buttermilk

2 tsp salt

50g (2oz) butter, plus extra for greasing

100g (4oz) fresh white breadcrumbs

40g (1½oz) freshly grated Parmesan

4 large slices chargrilled sourdough bread, to serve

snipped fresh chives, to garnish

tomato or chilli relish, to serve

CELERIAC SLAW:

1 small celeriac (about 675g (1½lb) in total)

4 tbsp roughly chopped fresh flat-leaf parsley

2 tbsp snipped fresh chives

2 tbsp buttermilk

1 tbsp maple syrup

2 tsp Dijon mustard

1 tsp cider vinegar

120ml (4fl oz) mayonnaise

sea salt and freshly ground black pepper

Putting chicken in buttermilk is a wonderful way to quickly tenderise it and make the flesh much more succulent. If you had the time you could leave it in the buttermilk overnight, but 15 minutes at room temperature really does make a difference.

Cut each chicken fillet in half into 2 thin escalopes. Place on a chopping board, put a piece of non-stick parchment paper on top of each one and quickly flatten out with a rolling pin to about 1cm (½in) thick. Place the buttermilk and salt in a bowl and add the chicken. Set aside at room temperature for at least 15 minutes to allow the buttermilk to tenderise the chicken, or place in the fridge overnight if you have the time.

Meanwhile, to make the celeriac slaw, peel the celeriac and then cut into julienne on a mandolin. Whisk the parsley, chives, buttermilk, maple syrup, mustard and vinegar into the mayonnaise and then fold in the celeriac. Season to taste.

Preheat the grill to high. Melt the butter in a small pan or in the microwave, then tip into a bowl. Add the breadcrumbs and Parmesan and season to taste, then mix well to combine. Remove the chicken from the buttermilk marinade, gently shaking off any excess. Place on a greased baking sheet and top with the breadcrumb mixture. Grill for 4–5 minutes, until the chicken is cooked through and the crumbs are golden.

Arrange the celeriac slaw on the chargrilled sourdough on warmed plates. Top with the crispy buttermilk chicken and scatter over the chives. Serve at once with small dishes of tomato or chilli relish for dipping.

CREAMY CHICKEN KORMA

SERVES 4

2 tbsp rapeseed oil

2 onions, finely chopped

2 garlic cloves, crushed

1 green chilli, seeded and finely chopped (optional)

2 tsp finely grated root ginger

1 tsp garam masala

1 tsp ground turmeric

¼ tsp chilli powder

400g (14oz) can chopped tomatoes

2 tbsp mango chutney, plus extra to serve

1 tsp tomato purée

400g (14oz) can coconut milk

4 x 175g (6oz) boneless, skinless chicken breasts, cut into 2.5cm (1in) cubes

sea salt and freshly ground black pepper

steamed basmati rice, to serve

handful of fresh coriander leaves, to garnish

warmed naan bread or green chilli and coriander flatbreads (page 242), to serve

The spicing in this korma is absolutely authentic, so it won't resemble the formula restaurant version. Apparently it is traditionally the emperor's favourite and it's now one of mine too. In India it would be garnished with fresh rose petals, but for me it needs nothing more than a scattering of fresh coriander leaves.

Heat the oil in a large pan over a medium-high heat and fry the onions and garlic for 6–8 minutes, until golden brown. Stir in the green chilli, if using, and the ginger and cook for 1 minute, stirring.

Add the garam masala to the pan with the turmeric, chilli powder and a pinch of salt and cook for another minute, stirring. Add the tomatoes, chutney, tomato purée and 4 tablespoons of water. Stir well to combine, then bring to a fast simmer for 5 minutes, until the sauce is so well reduced that it is almost sticking to the bottom of the pan, stirring occasionally.

Stir the coconut milk into the pan and then stir in the chicken. Slowly bring to the boil, then reduce the heat and simmer gently for 10–15 minutes, until the chicken is cooked through and completely tender. Season to taste.

To serve, arrange the basmati rice and chicken korma on warmed plates and scatter over the coriander leaves to garnish. Place the naan or green chilli and coriander flatbreads in a separate dish to pass around at the table along with the mango chutney.

PASTA

CHEAT'S GNOCCHI WITH TOMATO CREAM SAUCE AND PECORINO

SERVES 4

TOMATO CREAM SAUCE:

2 tbsp olive oil

1 small onion, finely chopped

400g (14oz) can good-quality Italian plum tomatoes

pinch of sugar

4 tbsp cream

GNOCCHI:

500g (1lb 2oz) fresh ricotta

150g (5oz) plain flour, sifted, plus extra for dusting

40g (1½oz) freshly grated Parmesan

2 eggs, lightly beaten

sea salt and freshly ground black pepper

Pecorino cheese shavings, to garnish

Regular gnocchi takes a bit of expertise and is probably something that most people will order when they're eating out or attempt to make for a special dinner. This version is almost foolproof and tastes great. It uses ricotta instead of potato, which makes it much easier to handle.

To make the tomato cream sauce, heat the oil over a medium heat in a small pan. Add the onion and sauté for 3–4 minutes, until softened but not coloured. Tip in the tomatoes and add the sugar and seasoning. Simmer for 4–6 minutes, stirring occasionally, until slightly reduced and thickened, then blitz with a hand blender until smooth and return to the pan.

Meanwhile, bring a large pan of salted water to a rolling boil. To make the gnocchi, place the ricotta, flour, Parmesan, eggs and ½ teaspoon of salt in a bowl. Mix well to combine, then divide the dough into 4 pieces and roll each piece on a lightly floured work surface into a rope 2cm (½in) wide and 30cm (12in) long, then cut into 2.5cm (1in) pieces.

Cook the gnocchi in small batches in the boiling water for 2–3 minutes, until the gnocchi are cooked through and floating on the surface. Drain well and keep warm.

To finish the tomato cream sauce, stir in the cream and allow to warm through but not to boil. Season to taste.

Divide the gnocchi among warmed wide-rimmed bowls and spoon over some of the tomato cream sauce. The rest can be served in a jug on the table. Add a grinding of black pepper and scatter over the Pecorino to serve.

PURPLE SPROUTING BROCCOLI PAPPARDELLE WITH GREMOLATA CRUMBS

SERVES 6–8

500g (1lb 2oz) good-quality pappardelle

500g (1lb 2oz) purple sprouting broccoli

100g (4oz) sourdough or crusty bread

2 garlic cloves, crushed

2 tbsp olive oil

50g (2oz) shelled walnuts, roughly chopped

finely grated rind of 1 small lemon

3 tbsp roughly chopped fresh flat-leaf parsley

2 tbsp extra virgin olive oil

50g (2oz) freshly grated Parmesan, plus extra to garnish

sea salt and freshly ground black pepper

This would also be delicious with a creamy blue cheese such as Dolcelatte instead of or even in addition to the Parmesan. It is a pasta dish that depends on very good ingredients but will have a fantastic supper on the table in 15 minutes.

Place the pappardelle in a large pan of boiling salted water and cook for 5–7 minutes or according to the packet instructions, until al dente.

Meanwhile, trim the florets off the purple sprouting broccoli and cut the tender stalks into slices on the diagonal.

Put the bread, garlic and olive oil in a food processor and season generously. Blitz in short bursts until it forms small crumbs. Heat a frying pan over a medium-high heat and sauté the crumbs and walnuts for 4–5 minutes, until golden. Remove from the heat and stir in the lemon rind and parsley.

Put the purple sprouting broccoli into a steamer and cook for 3–4 minutes, until quite tender – it should be cooked slightly more than usual.

Drain the pappardelle well, then return it to the pan and toss in the gremolata crumbs, extra virgin olive oil, Parmesan and steamed purple sprouting broccoli. Season to taste and divide among warmed bowls. Scatter over a little more Parmesan and a good grinding of black pepper to serve.

SPINACH AND RICOTTA LASAGNE WITH MOZZARELLA

SERVES 6–8

This is a fantastic lasagne that you can have on the table in no time at all. Choose the largest shop-bought ravioli you can find, as they will be easy to work with. It's also worth paying a little extra for the best cans of Italian plum tomatoes you can find. There really is a world of difference in the taste, and the richness of their flavour means you don't even need to use tomato purée. I promise you'll never look back.

Preheat the oven to 200°C (400°F/gas mark 6).

To make the tomato sauce, heat the oil in a wide pan over a medium heat and gently sauté the onion for a couple of minutes, until softened but not coloured. Tip in the tomatoes, then add the sugar and season to taste. Mash down with a potato masher, then bring to the boil and boil fast for about 5 minutes to reduce and thicken. Add the basil leaves, then blitz with a hand blender until smooth.

Cook the ravioli for 2–3 minutes in a large pan of boiling salted water or according to the packet instructions, then drain well. Arrange half of the ravioli in the bottom of a 2.5 litre (4½ pint) capacity ovenproof dish and cover with half of the tomato sauce. Add a layer of prosciutto slices and then repeat with the remaining ravioli, tomato sauce and prosciutto. Cover with the mozzarella and sprinkle the Parmesan on top.

Bake the lasagne in the oven for 15 minutes, then quickly flash under the grill until the mozzarella and Parmesan are bubbling and golden. Garnish with a few basil sprigs and serve straight to the table with a separate bowl of salad.

4 x 300g (11oz) packets of fresh spinach and ricotta ravioli

12 slices prosciutto

2 x 120g (4½oz) balls of buffalo mozzarella, sliced (Toonsbridge if possible)

25g (1oz) freshly grated Parmesan

lightly dressed mixed salad, to serve

TOMATO SAUCE:

2 tbsp olive oil

1 onion, finely chopped

2 x 400g (14oz) cans Italian plum tomatoes

good pinch of sugar

handful of fresh basil leaves, plus extra sprigs to garnish

sea salt and freshly ground black pepper

SPAGHETTI WITH SEAFOOD

SERVES 4

1.5kg (3¼lb) mussels

2 tbsp dry white wine

350g (12oz) spaghetti

4 tbsp extra virgin olive oil

2 garlic cloves, thinly sliced

1 red chilli, thinly sliced into rings

2 small squid, cleaned and cut into thin rings

350g (12oz) raw prawns, peeled and veins removed

200g (7oz) cherry tomatoes, halved

2 tbsp chopped fresh flat-leaf parsley

sea salt and freshly ground black pepper

This makes a nice change from your average bowl of pasta and is perfect when you want something special but don't have a lot of time on your hands. To save time, ask your fishmonger to prepare all the seafood for you. The prawns and squid can also be frozen. Add a couple of tablespoons of cream or crème fraîche for a richer sauce if you like.

Clean the mussels and remove the beards under cold running water. Place in a pan with a lid and pour over the wine. Cover tightly and cook over a high heat for a few minutes, shaking the pan occasionally, until all the mussels have opened – discard any that do not open. Strain through a sieve, reserving 150ml (¼ pint) of the cooking liquor, leaving behind any grit. Reserve a few mussels for garnish and remove the remainder from their shells.

Meanwhile, twirl the spaghetti into a pan of boiling salted water. Stir once and cook for 10–12 minutes or according to the instructions on the packet, until al dente.

Heat the oil in a heavy-based frying pan over a medium-high heat. Add the garlic and chilli and sauté for about 30 seconds, until lightly golden. Add the squid and continue to cook for a few minutes, then tip in the prawns and sauté for another minute or so, until just sealed. Add the reserved mussel cooking liquid and reduce slightly, then tip in the mussels, cherry tomato halves and parsley. Season to taste and allow to just warm through.

Drain the pasta and return it to the pan, then pour in the seafood sauce and stir together until well combined. Divide among warmed wide-rimmed bowls and serve at once.

PENNE WITH PUMPKIN, CRISPY PANCETTA, SAGE AND PARMESAN

SERVES 4–6

500g (1lb 2oz) penne or rigatoni

4 tbsp olive oil

175g (6oz) pancetta or smoked streaky bacon lardons

800g (1lb 12oz) small pumpkin, peeled, seeded and finely diced

4 tbsp finely shredded fresh sage

250g (9oz) carton mascarpone cheese (Kilbeg if possible)

50g (2oz) freshly grated Parmesan, plus extra to garnish

25g (1oz) toasted pine nuts

sea salt and freshly ground black pepper

Look for small organic pumpkins called Jack O Lantern, now grown all over Ireland. They are a vibrant orange and they are the ideal size for this recipe. Once the pumpkin is peeled and seeded you should end up with just over 450g (1lb) of diced flesh, the perfect amount to feed a family.

Bring a large pan of salted water to the boil. Add the penne or rigatoni and cook for 10–12 minutes or according to the packet instructions, until al dente.

Heat a large heavy-based pan with the olive oil, then add the pancetta or smoked streaky bacon lardons. Cook for 2–3 minutes, stirring occasionally, until the pancetta begins to go crispy. Remove with a slotted spoon and set aside until needed.

Add the pumpkin to the pan with the sage and mix well to combine. Season to taste and cook for 8–10 minutes, stirring occasionally, until the pumpkin is cooked through but still holding its shape. Stir in the mascarpone and simmer for 1–2 minutes.

Drain the pasta and add to the pumpkin with the reserved crispy pancetta. Stir in the Parmesan and season to taste. Divide among warmed wide-rimmed bowls and finish each one with a sprinkling of Parmesan and a good grinding of black pepper. Sprinkle over the pine nuts to serve.

DINNER
PARTY

LAMB TAGLIATA WITH PUY LENTIL AND GOAT'S CHEESE SALAD

SERVES 8

1 tbsp chopped fresh rosemary

1 tsp sea salt

1 tsp freshly ground black pepper

1.75kg (3lb 12oz) butterflied leg of lamb, well trimmed – ask the butcher to make sure no piece is thicker than 5cm (2in)

2 tbsp olive oil

roughly chopped fresh flat-leaf parsley, to garnish

PUY LENTIL SALAD:

4 tbsp extra virgin olive oil

4 shallots, finely chopped

2 x 400g (14oz) cans Puy lentils, drained and rinsed

100g (4oz) sun-dried tomatoes (preserved in oil), drained and chopped

350g (12oz) goat's cheese log, cut into bite-sized pieces

25g (1oz) fresh flat-leaf parsley leaves, roughly chopped

sea salt and freshly ground black pepper

In Italy, tagliata means 'cut'. Italians cleverly serve their meat thinly sliced and shared, turning a heavy meat dish into something lighter, brighter and more like a salad. It is as great to eat in the winter as it is in the summer, when the lamb could be done on the barbecue.

Preheat the oven to 220°C (425°F/gas mark 7).

Mix together the rosemary, sea salt and pepper. Rub the butterflied leg of lamb with the oil and then press in the rosemary seasoning. Put the leg of lamb on a rack set over a large roasting tin, skin side up, and roast for 25 minutes for medium rare or until cooked to your liking. Rest the lamb in a warm place for a few minutes loosely covered with foil.

Meanwhile, to make the salad, heat 1 tablespoon of the olive oil in a pan and sauté the shallots for 4–5 minutes, until softened but not coloured. Tip into a bowl and stir in the Puy lentils with the remaining 3 tablespoons of the olive oil and the sun-dried tomatoes. Gently fold in the goat's cheese and parsley, then season to taste. Arrange in a large salad bowl.

To serve, carve the rested butterflied leg of lamb into thin slices and arrange on a board, then drizzle over any meat juices. Scatter over the parsley and serve at once with the lentil salad.

STICKY GLAZED PORK FILLET WITH ASIAN GREENS IN PARCHMENT

SERVES 4

4 x 100g (4oz) pieces pork fillet, well trimmed

2 tbsp dark soy sauce

2 tbsp hoisin sauce

1 tbsp tomato ketchup

1 tbsp sweet sherry

1 tbsp honey

2 tsp dark muscovado sugar

5cm (2in) piece root ginger, peeled and cut into fine strips (julienne)

4 star anise

steamed Thai fragrant rice, to serve

ASIAN GREENS:

4 pak choy

2 spring onions, trimmed and shredded

2 garlic cloves, cut into wafer-thin slices

1 mild red chilli, seeded and very thinly sliced

2.5cm (1in) piece root ginger, peeled and cut into fine strips (julienne)

1 tbsp oyster sauce

1 tbsp dark soy sauce

1 tsp toasted sesame oil

The beauty of these parcels is that the main and side dishes cook alongside each other in the oven, leaving you with nothing to do except chat to your guests! They take very little time to prepare but can be made well in advance and then cooked to order, leaving no last-minute stress! Buy one large pork fillet and you'll have enough for this recipe.

Preheat the oven to 160°C (325°F/gas mark 3).

Cut 4 large sheets of parchment paper and place a piece of pork fillet in each one. Mix together the soy sauce, hoisin, tomato ketchup, sherry, honey and sugar. Spoon over the pork and then top each one with the ginger and star anise. Fold over the paper to enclose and form a parcel to seal. Place on a baking tray and cook in the oven for 10 minutes.

Meanwhile, prepare the Asian greens. Cut the pak choy into quarters. Cut another 4 sheets of parchment paper and divide the pak choy among them. Top with the spring onions, garlic, chilli, ginger, oyster sauce, soy sauce and sesame oil, then form into parcels and seal. Place on a tray with the pork and cook for another 15 minutes, or until the pork and pak choy are tender.

Divide the parcels onto warmed plates and bring straight to the table to allow guests to open them themselves. Serve with a separate bowl of Thai fragrant rice.

ROAST FILLET OF BEEF WITH WHITE BEAN MASH AND SAVOY CABBAGE

SERVES 4

This white bean mash is a great alternative to creamy mashed potatoes and every bit as moreish. I have served it here with some rare fillet of beef, making it a great dinner party dish. Savoy cabbage provides some excellent colour and texture to the dish, but you could always use another variety, such as York or January King, depending on what's available.

Preheat the oven to 220°C (425°F/gas mark 7).

Place 1 tablespoon of the olive oil in a shallow non-metallic dish. Add the rosemary and most of the thyme, then season generously with black pepper. Add the beef fillet, turning to coat.

Heat a heavy-based ovenproof frying pan until smoking hot. Add the beef fillet and cook for 2–3 minutes, turning regularly, until well sealed all over. Transfer to the oven and roast for another 20–25 minutes for medium rare; if you like your beef more well done, cook it for a little longer.

Meanwhile, place another 2 tablespoons of olive oil and half of the butter in a heavy-based pan. Add the onion and garlic and cook over a gentle heat for about 10 minutes, stirring occasionally, until well softened but not coloured. Add the caraway seeds and cook for 1 minute before stirring in the cannellini beans and cooking for a few more minutes, until heated through.

5 tbsp extra virgin olive oil

2 tsp finely chopped fresh rosemary

2 tsp finely chopped fresh thyme

675g (1½lb) piece beef fillet

50g (2oz) butter

1 onion, finely chopped

2 garlic cloves, crushed

good pinch of caraway seeds

2 x 400g (14oz) cans cannellini beans, drained and rinsed

1 small Savoy cabbage, cored and shredded

about 6 tbsp chicken stock

1 tbsp chopped fresh flat-leaf parsley

1 tbsp chopped fresh chives

sea salt and freshly ground black pepper

To sauté the cabbage, heat a wok or large frying pan over a medium-high heat and add the remaining 2 tablespoons of olive oil and the rest of the butter. Tip in the cabbage with the rest of the thyme and sauté for 1–2 minutes, until softened but not coloured. Pour in a couple of tablespoons of the stock, season generously and allow to cook for another few minutes, stirring until almost all of the liquid has evaporated.

Stir the rest of the stock into the bean mixture and then mash to a rough mash consistency using a potato masher or fork. Fold in the parsley and chives, then season to taste.

Carve the beef into thin slices. Divide the bean mash among the warmed plates and arrange the carved beef fillet on top, drizzling over any juices from the pan. Add a mound of cabbage to each one to serve.

SEAFOOD STEW WITH TOMATOES AND FENNEL

SERVES 6–8

This is a fish stew with origins all over Italy. It is fantastic to make if you want to feed a crowd and tastes absolutely delicious. The base for the sauce can be made a couple of days in advance, ready to be cooked with the seafood and fish to order, leaving you with very little to do last minute.

Heat the extra virgin olive oil in a very large heavy-based pan over a medium heat. Add the fennel, onion, shallots and fennel seeds and sauté for about 5 minutes, until the onion is translucent. Add the garlic and chilli, then stir in the chopped tomatoes, tomato purée, orange rind, stock, wine and bay leaf. Season with salt, then cover and bring to a simmer. Reduce the heat to medium-low and simmer for about 10 minutes, until the flavours have blended together.

Add the red pepper and clams to the tomatoes and vegetables. Cover and cook for about 5 minutes, until the clams begin to open. Add the prawns, fish and crab claws. Simmer gently until the fish and prawns are just cooked through and the clams are completely open. Stir in the basil and cook gently for another 5 minutes (discard any clams that do not open). Season to taste and ladle the stew into warmed bowls and scatter over the reserved fennel fronds. Serve with grilled slices of sourdough bread on the side.

3 tbsp extra virgin olive oil

1 fennel bulb, trimmed (reserve the fronds for garnish) and thinly sliced

1 onion, thinly sliced

2 shallots, sliced

1 tsp fennel seeds

2 large garlic cloves, finely chopped

1 red chilli, seeded and finely chopped

400g (14oz) can chopped tomatoes

2 tbsp tomato purée

1 piece pared orange rind

300ml (½ pint) fresh fish stock

150ml (¼ pint) dry white wine

1 bay leaf

1 red pepper, seeds removed and sliced into batons

225g (8oz) large clams, cleaned

400g (14oz) raw prawns, peeled and deveined

225g (8oz) assorted firm-fleshed fish fillets, such as hake or monkfish, cut into 4cm (1½in) chunks

150g (5oz) crab claws (no shell)

2 tbsp shredded fresh basil

sea salt and freshly ground black pepper

grilled slices of sourdough bread, to serve

TWICE-BAKED CHEESE SOUFFLÉS WITH ROASTED BEETROOT

SERVES 8

25g (1oz) unsalted butter, plus extra for greasing

2 tbsp plain flour

120ml (4fl oz) milk

6 egg whites plus 4 egg yolks

600ml (1 pint) cream

¼ tsp fresh thyme leaves

225g (8oz) Gruyère cheese, coarsely grated

ROASTED BEETROOT:

8 cooked beetroot (from a vac-pack)

½ tsp fresh thyme leaves

2 tbsp olive oil

1 tsp balsamic vinegar

sea salt and freshly ground black pepper

This is a great vegetarian main course that will keep everyone happy. It can also be made up to a day in advance, ready to cook off the second time once your guests are seated. The beetroot helps to cut through the richness of the cream and cheese and makes the prefect accompaniment.

Preheat the oven to 200°C (400°F/gas mark 6).

Cut the beetroot into small even-sized wedges and place in a baking tin with the thyme. Drizzle over the olive oil and balsamic vinegar and toss to coat. Season to taste and roast for 15–20 minutes, until slightly caramelised around the edges, tossing occasionally to prevent them from burning.

Meanwhile, to make the twice-baked cheese soufflés, butter 8 x 12.5cm (5in) squares of parchment paper and place on a buttered baking sheet.

Place the butter, flour and milk in a small pan and bring to the boil, whisking continuously. Season to taste, reduce the heat and simmer for another 2–3 minutes, until you have a smooth, thick sauce. Remove from the heat.

Whisk the egg whites until stiff peaks form. Stir the egg yolks into the sauce, then remove 2 tablespoons of the sauce, cover and set aside until needed.

Transfer the remaining sauce to a large bowl and fold in one-third of the egg whites to loosen the mixture, then carefully fold in the rest. Divide the mixture between the buttered squares of parchment and bake for 5–6 minutes, until well risen and firm to the touch.

Meanwhile, heat the cream and thyme in a large ovenproof frying pan and season generously. Whisk in the reserved sauce and bring to a gentle simmer. Remove the soufflés from the oven, carefully peel off the parchment paper and slide them into the cream. Spoon some of the cream mixture on top and then sprinkle with the Gruyère. Put the frying pan back in the oven and bake for 5 minutes, until the soufflés are puffed up and lightly golden.

Transfer the soufflés to warmed wide-rimmed bowls and spoon around the sauce. Serve with the roasted beetroot on the side.

Twice-baked Cheese Soufflés with Roasted Beetroot

VEGETABLE
SIDES

BEETROOT BARLEY RISOTTO WITH GOAT'S CHEESE

SERVES 4–6

2 tbsp olive oil

1 onion, finely chopped

600ml (1 pint) vegetable stock
(from a cube is fine)

225g (8oz) pearl barley

½ tsp chopped fresh thyme

4 tbsp dry white wine

225g (8oz) cooked beetroot
(vac-packed and not in vinegar)

5 tbsp soured cream

175g (6oz) soft goat's cheese, cut
into small cubes

1 tbsp snipped fresh chives

sea salt and freshly ground
black pepper

This recipe uses pearl barley, which most Irish households will be familiar with, but here I use it to make something that more resembles an Italian risotto. It's a great dish to have tucked away in the fridge around the festive period and can be reheated easily with a little extra soured cream – just include the goat's cheese and chives at the end. I also like it with leftover roast beef, but it is also fantastic alongside cold turkey, ham or even pork.

Heat the oil in a large heavy-based frying pan over a high heat and sauté the onion for a couple of minutes to soften. Bring the vegetable stock to a simmer in a separate pan.

Stir the barley and thyme into the sautéed onion and cook for 1 minute, stirring. Pour in the wine and allow it to bubble down immediately, then pour in the simmering stock and give everything a good stir. Season to taste, then cover, reduce the heat and simmer for 20 minutes, until the barley is almost cooked through but still has a bit of a bite to it.

Meanwhile, place half of the beetroot in a food processor with the soured cream and blend to a purée. Dice the remainder and set aside until needed.

When the barley is cooked to your satisfaction, fold in the beetroot purée with the diced beetroot and turn into a warmed serving dish. Scatter over the goat's cheese and chives and add a good grinding of black pepper to serve.

GARLIC MASHED POTATOES

SERVES 4—6

1.5kg (3¼lb) floury potatoes (such as Rooster), peeled and cut into even-sized chunks

6 garlic cloves, peeled

120ml (4fl oz) milk

75g (3oz) butter

sea salt and freshly ground black pepper

snipped fresh chives, to garnish

This is a brilliant mashed potato recipe, which once mastered can be adapted for different results. Try replacing a couple of tablespoons of the milk with crème fraîche or cream for a richer version. A couple of tablespoons of chives or a good dollop of Dijon mustard can also work well, depending on what you are serving them with.

Place the potatoes in a large pan of salted water. Bring to the boil, cover and simmer for 15–20 minutes, or until the potatoes are tender without breaking up. Drain and return to the pan over a low heat to dry out.

Meanwhile, place the garlic in a small pan with the milk and simmer very gently for about 10 minutes, until completely softened, then blitz to a thick purée with a hand blender.

Mash the potatoes or pass them through a potato ricer or vegetable mouli if you want a really smooth finish. Using a wooden spoon, beat in the butter until melted and then beat in the warm garlic and milk purée until you have a smooth, creamy mash. Season to taste and garnish with the chives to serve.

SWEET POTATO WEDGES

SERVES 4

These potato wedges are a great way to get children to eat a more unusual vegetable. Orange-fleshed sweet potatoes are actually one of the best sources of beta-carotene and they have a superior ability to raise our blood levels of vitamin A. This benefit is particularly true for children. Give them a try, you won't be disappointed.

500g (1lb 2oz) sweet potatoes, peeled and cut into wedges

1 tbsp olive oil

½ tsp Cajun seasoning (optional)

sea salt and freshly ground black pepper

Preheat the oven to 200°C (400°F/gas mark 6).

Put the sweet potatoes on a baking sheet, drizzle with the olive oil and sprinkle over the Cajun seasoning, if using. Toss until evenly coated, then season to taste and roast for about 25 minutes, until cooked through and lightly golden. Serve hot.

CURLY KALE WITH CHORIZO AND ALMONDS

SERVES 4

250g (9oz) cooking chorizo, diced
50g (2oz) skinned whole almonds
250g (9oz) curly kale
a little groundnut or sunflower oil
1 garlic clove, crushed
sea salt and freshly ground
black pepper

Kale is one of those vegetables that was never regarded as being glamorous but is now the height of fashion and can be seen on many restaurant menus. This would also make a delicious topping for grilled bread, drizzled with the chorizo oil.

Heat a non-stick sauté pan or wok over a moderate heat. Add the chorizo and fry for 4–5 minutes, until golden. Lift out the chorizo with a slotted spoon onto a dish lined with kitchen paper. Reserve the oil that has come out of the chorizo to use in another dish (see above) and wipe the frying pan clean. Add the almonds to the heated frying pan and cook for 2–3 minutes, until pale gold, then lift out and add to the chorizo.

Meanwhile, wash the kale thoroughly. The leaves can hold grit in their curls. Put several of the leaves on top of one another and shred them coarsely, discarding the really thick ends of the stalks as you go.

Heat a little oil in the sauté pan or wok over a medium-high heat. Add the crushed garlic and shredded curly kale and cook for a couple of minutes, turning the greens over as they cook, until the kale is glossy and starting to darken in colour. Return the chorizo and almonds to the pan, add a little salt and pepper and continue cooking until everything is sizzling. Serve immediately.

CREAMED SPINACH

SERVES 4–6

1 tbsp olive oil

large knob of butter

1 onion, cut into wafer-thin slices

4 garlic cloves, cut into
wafer-thin slices

1 vine-ripened tomato, peeled,
seeded and diced

good pinch of freshly
grated nutmeg

450g (1lb) frozen spinach

150ml (¼ pint) cream

50g (2oz) dried white
breadcrumbs

50g (2oz) freshly grated Parmesan

sea salt and freshly ground
white pepper

There is no doubt that the best creamed spinach is made with frozen spinach, as it is more dense and has much less liquid in it. This makes for a fantastic freezer stand-by, which is delicious with almost anything, including leftover turkey and ham at Christmas.

Preheat the grill to high. Put the oil into a large pan over a medium heat and add the butter. Add the onion and garlic and cook for about 5 minutes, until softened but not coloured. Add the tomato and season to taste, then add the nutmeg. Cook for another few minutes, until the tomato has broken down a little and softened.

Add the spinach and cream to the tomato and onion mixture. Cover with a lid and simmer gently for 10–12 minutes, stirring occasionally, until the spinach has defrosted and softened. Tip into a 1 litre (1¾ pint) ovenproof dish that is approximately 15cm x 25.5cm (6in x 10in) and 4cm (1½in) deep. Scatter over the breadcrumbs and Parmesan and place under the grill for another 6–8 minutes, until bubbling and golden. Serve immediately straight to the table.

LEFTOVERS

SHEPHERD'S PIE

SERVES 4

1 tbsp olive oil

4 carrots, diced

1 onion, chopped

2 smoked bacon rashers, rind removed and diced

2 tbsp plain flour

1 tbsp Worcestershire sauce

300ml (½ pint) lamb or beef stock (or leftover gravy – see intro)

1 tbsp tomato purée

1 tsp chopped fresh thyme

450g (1lb) leftover cooked lamb, well trimmed and diced

1 tbsp chopped fresh flat-leaf parsley

buttered peas, to serve

CHEESY MASH:

900g (2lb) floury potatoes, peeled and cut into cubes

50g (2oz) mature Cheddar cheese, grated

25g (1oz) butter

100ml (3 ½fl oz) milk

sea salt and freshly ground black pepper

This recipe is a great way to get a second day's dinner out of a roast joint of lamb. It's bulked out with vegetables and you can also use up any leftover gravy you might have – simply replace the amount you have for the same quantity of stock and you might not even need to use flour as a thickener.

To make the cheesy mash, place the potatoes in a steamer and cook for 10–12 minutes, or until tender.

Meanwhile, heat a large pan over a medium heat and add the oil. Cook the carrots and onion for 4–5 minutes, until just changing colour. Tip in the smoked bacon and sauté for a few minutes, until lightly golden. Sprinkle over the flour and cook for another minute, stirring continuously.

Stir the Worcestershire sauce into the vegetables, then add the stock (or gravy), tomato purée and thyme. Mix well to combine, then fold in the lamb. Reduce the heat to low and simmer for 10 minutes, until the lamb has heated through and the sauce has nicely thickened. Finally, stir in the parsley and season to taste.

Preheat the grill to high. Place the cooked lamb and vegetable mixture into an ovenproof dish and keep warm. To finish the cheesy mash, mash the steamed potatoes well, making sure there are no lumps. Beat in the Cheddar cheese, butter and milk and season to taste. Gently spoon the cheesy mash on top of the lamb and vegetables, spreading it with the back of a spoon. Flash under the grill for 5–6 minutes, until bubbling and golden. Serve straight to the table with a separate bowl of buttered peas so that everyone can help themselves.

TO GARNISH:

handful of fresh mint and
basil leaves

thinly sliced spring onions

red chillies

chilli oil

When the wontons are ready and the coconut broth has simmered down sufficiently, carefully add the wontons in batches and cook gently for 2–3 minutes, until just cooked through. Transfer to a large tray with a slotted spoon. Add the fish sauce and lime juice to taste to the coconut broth and stir gently for just a few seconds, then blitz with a hand blender. Skim off the foam with a spoon into a bowl and reserve as a garnish.

Divide the cooked wontons among warmed bowls and ladle over the coconut broth. Carefully spoon over the reserved foam, then garnish with the mint and basil leaves, spring onions and chillies. Drizzle over the chilli oil to serve.

COLD ROAST BEEF WITH BEETROOT SOURED CREAM

SERVES 4

500g (1lb 2 oz) leftover rare roast beef, well trimmed and cut into thin slices

jacket potatoes
(see intro), to serve

lightly dressed watercress salad,
to serve

BEETROOT SOURED CREAM:
200ml (7fl oz) soured cream

1 tsp Dijon mustard

pinch of sugar

1 small raw beetroot

2 tbsp grated horseradish
(fresh or from a jar is fine)

sea salt and freshly ground
black pepper

The beetroot soured cream is a wonderful condiment to serve with cold roast beef. It's the kind of thing I love having tucked away in the fridge at Christmas to make a delicious, relaxed, easy dinner. If you're very short of time, cut a criss-cross into the top of each jacket potato and microwave on full power for about 8 minutes, then split in half, add a knob of butter and flash under a hot grill to lightly toast. I love my roast beef quite rare, but that of course is a personal preference.

To make the beetroot sauce, place the soured cream in a bowl and mix in the mustard and sugar. Using disposable vinyl gloves, peel the beetroot and horseradish, then using a microplane, finely grate them into the soured cream. Mix well to combine and season to taste, then transfer to a serving bowl.

Arrange the slices of cold roast beef on plates with the jacket potatoes topped with a pinch of salt, a knob of butter and a good grinding of black pepper. Add some watercress salad to the side and put the bowl of beetroot soured cream on the table so that everyone can help themselves.

QUICK CASSOULET

SERVES 4

This is an excellent shortcut version of the classic rich, slow-cooked casserole from the south of France. It's a brilliant way of using up the leftovers from a festive duck or goose Christmas feast that literally takes no time at all to prepare. I like it with plenty of sourdough bread to mop up all the delicious juices and perhaps a nice fresh green salad – what more could you want?

Preheat the oven to 220°C (425°F/gas mark 7). Grease a 1 litre (1¾ pint) oval gratin dish that is about 23cm (9in) x 15cm (6in) and 5cm (2in) deep with a little of the duck or goose fat.

Put the chorizo into a large bowl with the beans, duck or goose meat, garlic, parsley, thyme and seasoning. Mix to combine and then tip into the dish, drizzle over the gravy and scatter the bread-crumbs on top.

Melt the rest of the duck or goose fat in a small pan or in the microwave and drizzle over the breadcrumbs to keep them moist. Bake for 20–25 minutes, until bubbling and golden brown. Serve straight to the table with separate bowls of bread and salad so that everyone can help themselves.

3 tbsp duck or goose fat

250g (9oz) raw chorizo sausages, cut into bite-sized chunks

2 x 400g (14oz) cans cannellini beans, drained and rinsed

350g (12oz) leftover cooked duck (Silverhill) or goose meat, chopped into bite-sized pieces

2 garlic cloves, finely chopped

3 tbsp roughly chopped fresh flat-leaf parsley

1 tsp soft thyme leaves

300ml (½ pint) leftover duck or goose gravy

50g (2oz) fresh white breadcrumbs

sea salt and freshly ground black pepper

sourdough bread, to serve

lightly dressed green salad, to serve

LUNCHBOX

CLEVER LUNCHBOX IDEAS

As we all know, healthy lunch ideas that inspire you to put together real food for your kids are essential if you want your children to have a balanced diet. Packing a lunch into a sectioned lunchbox or small Tupperware containers makes it easy to put together an assortment of healthy bits of food in a way that is appealing to a small child's eye. It's important to include lots of textures, colours and a well-rounded assortment of food groups. Try to vary what you put in so that you don't pack the same thing every day.

SOME MENU SUGGESTIONS:

Melon ball skewers (using different varieties)

Cheese cubes with red and green grapes on skewers

Banana wrap – smear vanilla yoghurt on a wholemeal wrap,
put in a peeled banana,
then roll up to enclose and cut into quarters

Mini wholemeal pittas filled with lettuce, turkey,
tomato relish and cherry tomatoes

Baby carrots

Roasted red pepper hummus (shop-bought or homemade)

Bread sticks wrapped in thinly sliced baked ham or Parma ham

Crunchy soya beans

Dried apricots and cranberries

Mixed berry smoothie

BENTO BOXES

Bento boxes, which originate from Japan, are suddenly all the rage. Cuteness is the name of the game in the current trend of making bento lunches: food is often shaped into animals, flowers or cartoon characters. Although these adorable feasts tend to take a bit longer than a regular packed lunch, your child's reaction will be worth it. Whether you decide to go super cool or not, you'll need to purchase a bento box, which are now readily available in supermarkets and department stores.

CHOOSE AT LEAST ONE OPTION FROM EACH GROUP:

Strawberries

Raspberries

Blueberries

Seedless grapes

Mandarin orange segments

Cherries

Cubes of chicken

Chunks of their favourite cheese

Rolls of ham

Canned tuna flakes

Shredded cooked turkey

Pasta with tomato dipping saucepot

Crackers

Tortilla wraps

Bagel chips

Mini pitta pockets

Carrot batons

Slices of cucumber

Raw sugar snap peas or mangetout

Celery sticks

Handful of sweetcorn

A few cherry tomatoes

CHILLI BEAN TACOS

SERVES 4

This is a great dish to bring in a wide flask with all the other elements separate so that you can build the tacos wherever you're having your lunch. You could also serve it for supper and then give the leftovers to one lucky person in their lunchbox.

Heat the oil in a large pan over a medium heat. Add the onion, celery, garlic and chilli and cook for 10 minutes, until softened and lightly golden, scraping the bottom to remove any sediment. Stir in the spices and continue to cook for 1–2 minutes.

Stir in the beans, tomatoes, tomato purée and cocoa powder. Bring to the boil, then season to taste and simmer for 10–15 minutes, until well reduced and thickened, stirring occasionally to ensure that the bottom doesn't stick.

Meanwhile, make the tomato and avocado salsa. Place the tomatoes, avocado, coriander and lime juice in a bowl and season to taste. Mix well to combine.

To serve, place some of the chilli bean mixture into each taco shell and spoon the salsa on top. Add a dollop of soured cream to each one, garnish with the coriander sprigs and serve with lime wedges.

2 tbsp olive oil

1 onion, finely chopped

1 celery stick, diced

2 garlic cloves, finely chopped

1 red chilli, seeded and finely chopped

1 tsp ground cumin

1 tsp hot paprika

½ tsp ground coriander

400g (14oz) can haricot beans, drained and rinsed

400g (14oz) can kidney beans in chilli sauce

400g (14oz) can chopped tomatoes

1 heaped tbsp tomato purée

1 tsp unsweetened cocoa powder

8 crisp taco shells

200ml (7fl oz) carton soured cream

fresh coriander sprigs, to garnish

lime wedges, to serve

TOMATO AND AVOCADO SALSA:

2 ripe tomatoes, seeded and diced

1 ripe avocado, halved, stoned and diced

good handful of fresh coriander leaves, roughly chopped

juice of ½ lime

sea salt and freshly ground black pepper

SESAME CHICKEN PATTIES WITH CUCUMBER SALAD

SERVES 4

450g (1lb) minced chicken

25g (1oz) fresh white breadcrumbs

2 spring onions, finely chopped

2 tbsp sweet chilli sauce, plus extra to serve

2 tbsp chopped fresh coriander

50g (2oz) sesame seeds

2 tbsp sunflower oil

sweet chilli sauce, to serve

CUCUMBER SALAD:

1 mini cucumber

2 tbsp rice wine vinegar

2 tsp caster sugar

sea salt and freshly ground black pepper

This is a great lunchbox for adults and children alike. However, if it's going into a school, you'll need to check to see if they're allowed to bring in sesame seeds. They would also make a lovely picnic, as they are so transportable. Don't be tempted to overcook them, as they will become dry once they cool down – the key is succulence!

To make the sesame chicken patties, place the chicken, breadcrumbs, spring onions, chilli sauce and coriander in a bowl and mix well to combine. Season to taste and shape into 12 small patties. Put the sesame seeds on a plate and press the seeds into both sides of the patties.

Heat the oil in a large sauté pan and shallow fry the sesame chicken patties over a medium to high heat for 3–4 minutes on each side, until cooked through and golden. Drain on kitchen paper.

Meanwhile, pare the cucumber into long, thin ribbons and place in a bowl. Mix the vinegar and sugar together until the sugar has dissolved and then use to dress the cucumber.

To serve, pack the sesame chicken patties in a heatproof lunchbox with a separate pot of the pickled cucumber and a sealed dipping bowl of sweet chilli sauce.

SINGAPORE NOODLES

SERVES 4

12 dried Chinese mushrooms

2 heaped tbsp Chinese
dried shrimps

2 tbsp light soy sauce

2 tbsp dry sherry

225g (8oz) rice noodles

2 tbsp groundnut oil

1 large onion, finely chopped

2 garlic cloves, finely chopped

1 tbsp freshly grated root ginger

1 tbsp Madras curry powder (hot)

good pinch of salt

100g (4oz) cooked skinless
chicken or pork fillet,
finely shredded

100g (4oz) cooked peeled
prawns, chopped

1 bunch spring onions, trimmed
and finely chopped

This is one of those dishes that is worth taking a trip to the Asian su-permarket for, where you'll find Chinese dried mushrooms and shrimps, not to mention a fantastic range of rice noodles to choose from. The finished result will taste better than any Chinese takeaway. If you can't get them, use fresh shiitake mushrooms instead of dried ones and add in a few more fresh prawns.

Place the dried mushrooms and shrimps in a bowl and pour over the boiling water. Set aside for 15 minutes to soak. Drain the liquid, reserving 2 tablespoons, and place in a bowl with the soy sauce and sherry. Set aside until needed. Squeeze out the excess moisture from the mushrooms and chop into fine shreds.

Meanwhile, place the noodles in a large bowl, cover them with warm water and leave them to soak for 15 minutes, then drain well in a colander.

Heat the oil in a large wok or frying pan until very hot. Add the onion, garlic and ginger along with the shredded mushrooms and drained shrimps. Sauté for 5–6 minutes, until completely softened and all of the flavours have nicely combined.

Stir the curry powder and a pinch of salt into the onion mixture. Cook for another minute, stirring. Tip in the chicken or pork, prawns and spring onions, stirring quickly to combine. Add the drained noodles, then, using either a large fork or some chopsticks, toss the ingredients around so that everything is well combined.

Sprinkle the reserved mushroom and soy sauce mixture over the Singapore noodles, give everything a good stir and put into a wide-necked flask. Pack with chopsticks.

KIDS'
FAVOURITES

CHEESY NACHOS WITH AVOCADO AND SWEETCORN SALSA

SERVES 4

100g (4oz) canned or frozen sweetcorn kernels

1 ripe tomato, seeded and diced

1 ripe avocado, peeled, stoned and diced

4 spring onions, thinly sliced

25g (1oz) sliced jalapeño chillies, drained and chopped (from a jar or can)

225g (8oz) tortilla chips

4–5 tbsp soured cream

50g (2oz) Cheddar cheese, grated

sea salt and freshly ground black pepper

This is wicked comfort food at its best, perfect for a Saturday night with a good movie or a sleepover party. Use as much or as little toppings as you like and of course omit the jalapeño chillies if you don't fancy them.

Preheat the oven to 200°C (400°F/gas mark 6).

If using frozen sweetcorn, place it in a pan of boiling salted water and cook for a few minutes, until just tender, then drain and refresh under cold running water. Place in a large bowl with the tomato, avocado, spring onions and chillies. Stir to combine and season to taste.

Tip the tortilla chips into a shallow ovenproof dish and scatter the avocado and sweetcorn salsa on top. Spoon over the soured cream and finish with the Cheddar cheese. Bake for about 10 minutes, until the Cheddar is melted and bubbling. Serve at once straight from the dish.

SALMON FISHCAKES

SERVES 4–6

400g (14oz) salmon fillet

300ml (½ pint) milk

900g (2lb) leftover
mashed potatoes

1 bunch spring onions, trimmed
and thinly sliced

1 tbsp chopped fresh
flat-leaf parsley

4 tbsp plain flour

2 eggs, beaten

150g (5oz) fresh white or panko
breadcrumbs

4 tbsp sunflower oil

sea salt and freshly ground
black pepper

lightly dressed mixed salad,
to serve

mayonnaise, to serve

lemon wedges, to serve

Fishcakes are a great, easy way to introduce kids to fish. These are a favourite in our household. Feel free to add vegetables to the fishcakes: peas, carrots or sweetcorn would be good.

Place the salmon in a large pan. Pour over the milk, cover and bring to the boil. Remove from the heat and leave the fish for 5 minutes to finish cooking in the hot milk.

Put the mashed potatoes in a bowl and beat in the spring onions and parsley. Transfer the cooked salmon to a plate with a fish slice. Break up the flesh into rough flakes, discarding any skin and bones. Gently fold into the mashed potato mixture and season to taste. Using a small ice cream scoop, shape the salmon and potato mixture into 18 even-sized balls, then, using slightly wet hands, shape into patties.

Place the flour on a plate and season generously. Put the beaten eggs into a shallow dish and place the breadcrumbs in a separate dish. Dust the salmon fishcakes in the seasoned flour, carefully dip them in beaten egg and then coat in the breadcrumbs.

Heat the oil in a large heavy-based frying pan over a medium heat. Shallow fry the fishcakes in batches for 4–5 minutes on each side, until crisp and golden. Drain well on kitchen paper and then arrange on warmed plates with the mixed salad and a dollop of mayonnaise. Serve with the lemon wedges.

HAM, CHEESE AND EGG CRÊPES WITH GRIDDLED ASPARAGUS

SERVES 4–8

24 asparagus spears

8 eggs

450g (1lb) Swiss cheese, such as Gruyère or Emmental, thinly sliced

8 slices of cooked ham

1 tbsp olive oil

CRÊPES:

100g (4oz) plain flour

1 egg

300ml (½ pint) milk

sunflower oil, for frying

sea salt and freshly ground black pepper

This is a perfect tea for lots of hungry children, but it would also be a good weekend late breakfast, depending on your mood. It's the classic way that many crêpe stallholders cook crêpes to order late at night around the major tourist attractions in Paris. They are always very popular, often with long queues, and once you've tasted them it's easy to understand why.

Sift the flour and a pinch of salt into a bowl and make a well in the centre. Add the egg and whisk well with a balloon whisk. Gradually beat in the milk, drawing in the flour from the sides to make a smooth batter. Leave to rest for 5 minutes.

Meanwhile, trim the asparagus spears and blanch in a pan of boiling water for 1–2 minutes, until almost tender but still with a slight bite. Drain and refresh under cold running water to prevent them from cooking any further and set aside until needed.

Heat a little oil in an 18cm (7in) heavy-based pancake or frying pan. Pour in just enough batter to thinly coat the base of the pan. Cook over a moderately high heat for about 1 minute, until golden brown. Turn or toss the crêpe and break in an egg, then gently whisk to spread it evenly all over the crêpe. Season to taste.

Put a layer of cheese on half of the crêpe and allow it to melt for 30–60 seconds. Top with a slice of ham and flip in half, then flip into quarters and keep warm on a baking tray in a low oven loosely covered with foil while cooking the remainder. This mixture should make 8 ham, cheese and egg crêpes in total.

To finish the asparagus spears, heat a cast-iron griddle pan until smoking hot. Toss the blanched asparagus spears in the olive oil and season to taste. Add to the griddle pan and quickly sear on both sides, until heated through and lightly charred.

Arrange the ham, cheese and egg crêpes on warmed plates with the griddled asparagus and serve at once.

INSTANT STRAWBERRY ICE CREAM SUNDAE

SERVES 4

Watch children's faces light up as you make these ice cream sundaes before their very eyes! The ice cream is so much better for them than anything you can buy, contains so little fat and has a really fresh flavour. If there are any adults around, they'll be guaranteed to enjoy it just as much. Try using raspberries, which work just as well.

Roughly crush up the meringues into 4 sundae glasses. Cut the fresh strawberries into quarters and set aside until needed.

To make the ice cream, put the frozen strawberries into a food processor with the sugar, buttermilk and vanilla extract. Blitz until smooth and then quickly spoon over the crushed meringues. Top each one with a pile of fresh strawberries and decorate with the wafers. Serve at once.

4 meringues (homemade or shop-bought)
225g (8oz) fresh large strawberries
4 ice cream wafers

STRAWBERRY ICE CREAM:
400g (14oz) frozen strawberries
50g (2oz) caster sugar
150ml (¼ pint) buttermilk
½ tsp vanilla extract

CHOCOLATE COOKIE TOWER ICE CREAM CAKE

SERVES ABOUT 20

4 x 500ml (18fl oz) cartons vanilla ice cream

48 chocolate cookies (homemade, see page 226, or shop-bought)

8 chocolate flakes, finely chopped

8 Crunchie bars, finely chopped

This cake is fun to make with children for a birthday party or any special occasion. You can buy the chocolate cookies, or any large chocolate biscuit will work – just remember that the softer they are, the easier the cake will be to cut. You could also add layers of raspberries or strawberries or just use them to decorate.

Put half of the ice cream in a standalone mixer and whip it up so that it will be easier to manage. Arrange 8 cookies in a circle foundation on a cake stand. Working quickly and using a palette knife, spread over a layer of the softened ice cream and then sprinkle over some of the flake and Crunchies, making sure the cookies are still visible at the sides. Top with another layer of cookies.

Repeat the process, whipping the rest of the ice cream once you've run out. Continue the layers until you have used up all of the cookies and finish with a layer of the ice cream, making 6 layers each. Top with a final sprinkling of flakes and Crunchies. Serve immediately or put back into the freezer and chill down until needed.

DESSERTS

SUMMER FRUIT SABAYON

SERVES 4

3 egg yolks, beaten

50g (2oz) caster sugar

finely grated rind of ½ lemon

juice of 1 lemon

150ml (¼ pint) peach schnapps
or dry white wine

4 tbsp cream

450g (1lb) mixed summer fruit,
such as blueberries, raspberries,
stoned cherries, grapes and
apricot slices

I first remember making this classic French dessert in college and I can still taste how delicious it was. It's a wonderful showcase for the best fruit that summer can offer, so choose wisely and create a beautiful pattern of fruit on each plate – your guests will be well impressed!

Place the egg yolks and sugar in a heatproof bowl and beat until well combined. Add the lemon rind and juice along with the peach schnapps or wine, then set the bowl over a pan of simmering water (do not allow the bowl to touch the water).

Whisk the egg yolk mixture for 10–12 minutes, until the sabayon is smooth and has thickened, then gradually stir in the cream. Whisk for another minute until well combined.

Meanwhile, preheat the grill to high. Arrange the mixed summer fruits on shallow ovenproof plates or dishes, then pour over the sabayon and place under the grill for 6–8 minutes, until bubbling and golden. Serve at once.

CAPPUCCINO CREAM CHOCOLATE CAKE

SERVES 10–12

This might look like a very impressive cake that took ages to make, but it's really only an assembly job. Mascarpone is a rich, creamy cheese from Lodi in the Lombardy region of Italy. It has a sweetened taste and is famously used in classic tiramisu, which is the basis of this dessert. However, I've used shop-bought chocolate loaf cakes instead of the traditional sponge fingers.

Using an electric whisk, mix the mascarpone cheese, icing sugar and vanilla seeds until well combined. Whip 375ml (13fl oz) of the cream until soft peaks form and then fold into the mascarpone mixture.

Pour the coffee into a shallow dish and stir in the Coole Swan. Slice the chocolate loaves. Line the base and sides of a 23cm (9in) springform cake tin with parchment paper and wrap the outside in clingfilm to avoid any leaks.

Dip 8 of the chocolate cake slices in the Coole Swan mixture to cover the bottom of the tin. It's important to only dip them as you go along so that they are not soaking for long, which would make them difficult to handle.

Cover the layer of soaked chocolate cake with one-third of the mascarpone cream and then arrange another even layer of the soaked cake slices on top. Continue layering in this way, finishing with a mascarpone layer, and place in the fridge to chill for 10–15 minutes.

Meanwhile, whip the rest of the cream in a clean bowl and transfer to a piping bag fitted with a star-shaped nozzle. When ready to serve, carefully remove from the cake tin and transfer to a cake stand. Give the cake an even dusting of the cocoa powder, then pipe 10–12 peaks of cream around the edge of the cake and top each one with a chocolate-covered coffee bean. Place in the middle of the table so that everyone can help themselves.

750g (1¾lb) mascarpone cheese, well chilled

200g (7oz) icing sugar, sifted

1 vanilla pod, split in half and seeds scraped out

450ml (¾ pint) cream, well chilled

200ml (7fl oz) freshly brewed strong espresso coffee, left to cool

100ml (3½fl oz) Coole Swan Irish cream liqueur

2 x 380g (13oz) chocolate loaf cakes (shop-bought or homemade)

2 tsp good-quality cocoa powder

10–12 chocolate-covered coffee beans, to decorate

APRICOT PUDDING WITH AMARETTI CUSTARD

SERVES 4–6

butter, to grease

2 eggs, separated

50g (2oz) caster sugar

1 tsp vanilla extract

25g (1oz) ground almonds

50ml (2fl oz) milk

2 tbsp cream

2 x 400g (14oz) cans apricot halves, drained

icing sugar, to dust

amaretti custard, to serve (see intro)

This pudding is incredibly easy to make and should take no more than 5 minutes to get into the oven. It's a great store cupboard standby, or you could use fresh ripe apricots that have been skinned if they are in season. Just make sure they are very ripe or they will not cook in the time allowed. To make amaretti custard, simply whisk a couple of tablespoons of the liqueur into your favourite custard.

Preheat the oven to 200°C (400°F/gas mark 6). Butter a shallow ovenproof dish that has a 1.5 litre (2½ pint) capacity and is 30.5cm (12in) x 20cm (8in) and about 5cm (2in) deep.

Beat together the egg yolks, sugar and vanilla extract in a large bowl until foamy. Beat in the almonds, then the milk and cream. Whisk the egg whites very lightly in a separate bowl until they just begin to hold their shape, then carefully fold into the egg and sugar mixture.

Pour the mixture into the buttered ovenproof dish and arrange the apricot halves on top. Bake for 20–25 minutes, until just set. You may need to cover the pudding towards the end of the cooking time to prevent it from turning too brown. Dust with icing sugar and serve hot, straight to the table. Hand around a jug of warm amaretti custard separately.

PEACH TARTE TATIN WITH CITRUS MASCARPONE

SERVES 4

3 ripe peaches
50g (2oz) butter
50g (2oz) caster sugar
2 tbsp cream
1 tbsp brandy
320g (11oz) packet ready-rolled puff pastry, thawed if frozen

CITRUS MASCARPONE:
½ tsp finely grated orange rind
½ tsp finely grated lemon rind
100g (4oz) mascarpone cheese
2 tbsp fresh orange juice
1–2 tbsp sifted icing sugar

This is a very impressive dessert to get done in such a short time, but it's definitely achievable by using the ready-to-roll puff pastry. Look for the all-butter version, which more supermarkets are now stocking.

Preheat the oven to 220°C (425°F/gas mark 7) and preheat the grill.

Place the peaches in a pan of boiling water for 1 minute, remove with a slotted spoon, then plunge into cold water and peel away the skins. Cut into halves and remove the stones, then cut into quarters.

Meanwhile, melt the butter with the sugar in a small pan. Bring to the boil and simmer for 5–6 minutes, until thickened and lightly golden. Remove from the heat and leave to cool for 1 minute, then stir in the cream, beating until smooth. Spoon into a shallow 20cm (8in) sandwich tin. Arrange the peach quarters on top, cut side up, and drizzle over the brandy.

Unroll the puff pastry on a clean work surface and cut out a 25cm (10in) round. Place it over the peaches, pushing the edges down the side of the tin; trim off any excess pastry. Place on a baking sheet and bake for 15–20 minutes, until golden brown.

Meanwhile, to make the citrus mascarpone, beat the orange and lemon rind into the mascarpone and then stir in the orange juice. Add enough of the icing sugar to sweeten.

Preheat the grill to high (unless you have a kitchen blowtorch and can use that instead). Loosen the puff pastry from the tin with a knife. Cool, then turn out onto a heatproof dish and quickly gratinate the top under the grill or with a blowtorch until caramelised. Serve cut into slices on warmed plates with quenelles of the citrus mascarpone.

RASPBERRY SOUFFLÉS WITH VANILLA ICE CREAM

SERVES 4

400g (14oz) raspberries, plus extra to decorate

100g (4oz) caster sugar, plus extra to dust

1 vanilla pod, split in half and seeds scraped out

2 tbsp crème de cassis

1 tsp cornflour mixed with 1 tsp water

4 egg whites

unsalted butter, to grease

icing sugar, to dust

vanilla ice cream, to serve

This recipe was given to me by TV chef Nick Nairn, who also runs a lovely cookery school in Scotland. It is literally foolproof and guarantees perfect results every time. It also works brilliantly with blackcurrants because of their high pectin content.

Place the raspberries in a wide heavy-based pan with the caster sugar. Mash down with a hand-held masher until they start to release their juices, then add the vanilla seeds and crème de cassis. Allow to bubble on a high heat for about 10 minutes, stirring regularly, until you have achieved a jam-like consistency.

Pass the raspberry purée through a fine sieve into a bowl and then stir in the cornflour so that it thickens the purée slightly. Leave to cool.

When ready to cook the soufflés, preheat the oven to 180°C (350°F/gas mark 4). Generously grease 8 x 200ml (7fl oz) ramekins with butter and dust with caster sugar, shaking out any excess.

Whisk the egg whites in a clean, dry bowl until stiff, then fold into the thickened raspberry purée. Use to fill the prepared ramekins and level the tops with a palette knife.

Arrange the soufflés on a baking sheet and bake for 10–12 minutes, until well risen and golden brown on top. Dust with icing sugar and arrange on plates with a separate ramekin of vanilla ice cream and a row of raspberries. Serve at once.

BAKING

CHILLI AND CRAB CORNBREAD MUFFINS

MAKES 12

150g (5oz) self-raising flour

1 tbsp caster sugar

2 tsp baking powder

1 tsp salt

150g (5oz) yellow cornmeal
(maize meal)

½ tsp cracked black pepper

2 eggs, lightly beaten

50g (2oz) butter, melted

300ml (½ pint) cultured
buttermilk (or milk mixed with
the juice of ½ lemon)

200g (7oz) fresh white crabmeat

1 red chilli, seeded and
finely chopped

2 tbsp chopped fresh mixed herbs
(such as flat-leaf parsley,
chives and basil)

These taste best warm. They can be made up to one day in advance and stored in an airtight container in the fridge, then reheated in a warm oven for 5 minutes. Omit the crab for a vegetarian option. These also freeze very well for up to one month. To use, defrost at room temperature for 2 hours and reheat gently in a warm oven for about 5 minutes.

Preheat the oven to 180°C (350°F/gas mark 4). Line a 12-hole muffin tin with paper cases.

Sift the flour, sugar, baking powder and salt into a bowl, then stir in the cornmeal and pepper. Make a well in the centre of the dry ingredients and quickly stir in the eggs, melted butter and buttermilk until you have achieved a smooth batter. Fold in the crabmeat, chilli and herbs until just combined.

Spoon the mixture into the prepared muffin tin and bake for about 20 minutes, until the muffins are golden brown and a skewer comes out clean. Serve warm with soup or scrambled eggs as a late breakfast or brunch.

RASPBERRY AND LEMON CURD SPONGE

SERVES 6

knob of butter, for greasing

5 eggs, at room temperature

150g (5oz) caster sugar

175g (6oz) self-raising flour, sifted

1 tsp vanilla extract

120ml (4fl oz) lemon curd

250g (9oz) raspberries

icing sugar, to dust

This cake can be on the table in 20 minutes. It's delicious with any fresh fruit, such as raspberries, strawberries or even a drained can of peach slices – whatever you have to hand, really!

Preheat the oven to 180°C (350°F/gas mark 4). Lightly grease 2 x 20cm (8in) cake tins and line the bases with parchment paper.

Place the eggs and sugar in a large bowl. Using either a hand whisk or electric whisk, beat the mixture until it fills over half the bowl and has the consistency of lightly whipped cream. Using a dessert spoon, gently fold in the sifted flour one spoonful at a time until all the flour is fully absorbed, then beat in the vanilla extract.

Divide the batter between the prepared cake tins and bake for about 15 minutes. The cake is cooked when it comes slightly away from the tin. Turn out onto wire racks and leave to cool for as long as time allows.

To serve, spread the lemon curd on one side of the sponge, almost but not quite to the edge, and then cover with all but 3 of the raspberries. Carefully place the other sponge on top to cover the filling completely. Add a light dusting of icing sugar, decorate with the remaining 3 raspberries and place on a cake stand, then cut into slices to serve.

SOFT CHOCOLATE COOKIES

MAKES 24 BISCUITS

150g (5oz) plain chocolate drops
(preferably 70% cocoa solids)

120g (4½oz) butter

225g (8oz) caster sugar

3 large eggs

1 tsp vanilla extract

250g (9oz) plain flour

25g (1oz) good-quality
cocoa powder

½ tsp baking powder

If you want to serve these cookies straight away, they are delicious as a plain cookie with a cup of coffee or a couple scoops of your favourite ice cream. However, if time is on your side, try sandwiching them together with a vanilla buttercream to make the classic whoopie pie.

Preheat the oven to 180°C (350°F/gas mark 4). Line 2 large baking sheets with parchment paper.

Melt the chocolate and butter in a heatproof bowl set over a pan of barely simmering water. Remove from the heat and leave to cool slightly.

Whisk the sugar, eggs and vanilla in a separate bowl for about 3 minutes, until light, fluffy and pale in colour, then fold in the chocolate mixture.

Sift the flour, cocoa powder and baking powder into a bowl and then fold into the chocolate mixture. Place heaped tablespoons of the dough onto the lined baking sheets – the mixture should make 24 cookies. Bake for 10–12 minutes, until well risen and just set. Remove from the oven and leave to cool for a couple of minutes before removing from the tray, carefully peeling off the parchment paper. Serve warm or cold.

PEANUT BUTTER CUPCAKES WITH SALTED CARAMEL FROSTING

MAKES 12

My sister Sonya is mad into baking and is the inspiration behind these peanut butter cupcakes. If you want to really up the ante, decorate the salted caramel frosting with a thin drizzle of caramel, which is now readily available in all supermarkets.

Preheat the oven to 180°C (350°F/gas mark 4). Line a 12-hole muffin tin with paper cases.

Place the sugar, peanut butter and butter in a standalone mixer and beat until light and fluffy. Add the eggs one at a time, whisking continuously. Tip in the vanilla extract and continue mixing. The more you mix, the lighter it becomes.

Meanwhile, sift the flour and baking powder into a bowl. Add one-third of the flour to the sugar mixture and gently fold it in. Add one-third of the milk and fold it in, continuing in this way until all of the flour and milk are well combined. Scoop the batter into the lined muffin tin, filling each one no more than two-thirds full. Bake for 20–22 minutes, until well risen and golden.

To make the salted caramel frosting, beat the icing sugar and butter in a mixer until light and fluffy. Add the caramel, milk and salt and beat for another 4 minutes, until lightly and fluffy. Spoon into a piping bag fitted with a 2.5cm (1in) star-shaped nozzle.

Remove the cupcakes from the oven and if time allows, allow to cool. Otherwise, serve the cupcakes on plates with a little dish of piped frosting on the side. Give each guest a knife and allow them to spread on the frosting themselves.

200g (7oz) dark muscovado sugar

120g (4½oz) smooth peanut butter

75g (3oz) butter

2 large eggs

1 tsp vanilla extract

120g (4½oz) plain flour

1 tsp baking powder

50ml (2fl oz) milk

SALTED CARAMEL FROSTING:

350g (12oz) icing sugar, sifted

100g (4oz) unsalted butter

6 tbsp caramel or dulce de leche, from a can

2 tbsp milk

good pinch of sea salt flakes

OATMEAL, CRANBERRY AND WHITE CHOCOLATE COOKIES

MAKES ABOUT 12

275g (10oz) Flahavan's Progress Oatlets

225g (8oz) butter, at room temperature

150g (5oz) caster sugar

100g (4oz) plain flour, plus a little extra for dusting

½ tsp baking soda

100g (4oz) dried cranberries, roughly chopped

100g (4oz) white chocolate, finely chopped

The inspiration for this recipe was given to me by Mary Flahavan. I like it so much that we now make it up in batches and keep them in Kilner jars in our rooms for guests in case they're feeling a bit peckish after a long journey but don't want to ruin their dinner.

Preheat the oven to 200°C (400°F/gas mark 6). Line 2 baking sheets with parchment paper.

Blend the oatlets in a food processor until quite fine. Add the butter, sugar, flour and baking soda and blend again until the dough just comes together. Tip into a bowl and beat in the cranberries and white chocolate.

Shape into 12 even-sized balls and arrange on the lined baking sheets well spaced apart, then squash them down with the palm of your hand to about a 4cm (1½in) thickness. Bake for 15–20 minutes, until they are a pale golden colour and soft to the touch. Remove from the oven and leave to cool and harden on the sheets for a minute, then transfer to a wire rack and leave to cool for a few minutes before tucking in with a nice glass of milk or a cup of tea.

BREADS

POTATO FARLS

MAKES 8 FARLS

50g (2oz) butter, plus extra
for serving

500g (1lb 2oz) leftover
mashed potatoes

½ tsp salt

175g (6oz) plain flour, plus
extra for dusting

sunflower oil, for cooking

chopped fresh flat-leaf parsley,
to garnish

Traditionally potato farls have always been a great way of using a bowl of leftover mashed potatoes. They can be served with a good old fry-up or some bacon and eggs for a light supper. Just be careful not to overhandle the dough or it will become tough.

Melt the butter in a small pan or in the microwave. Put the leftover mashed potatoes into a bowl with the melted butter and salt and mash until smooth. Sift over the flour and then quickly work to a smooth dough. Knead very briefly on a lightly floured surface. Cut the dough in half and roll out to a 20cm (8in) round that is about 5mm (¼in) thick, then cut into quarters. Repeat with the remaining dough.

Heat a flat griddle or a large frying pan over a medium-high heat. Add a thin film of oil to the heated pan and cook a batch of the potato farls for 2–3 minutes on each side, until golden brown. Repeat until all of the potato farls have been cooked. Rub a little butter on each potato farl and arrange on a warmed plate. Garnish with the parsley to serve.

BROWN SCONES

MAKES ABOUT 10

rapeseed or sunflower oil,
for greasing

225g (8oz) self-raising flour, plus
extra for dusting

225g (8oz) coarse wholemeal flour

½ tsp baking soda

½ tsp salt

50g (2oz) wheat bran

25g (1oz) butter, diced and at
room temperature

1 tsp light muscovado sugar

300ml (½ pint) buttermilk, plus a
little extra if necessary

1 tsp golden syrup

butter or lightly whipped cream,
to serve

strawberry jam, to serve

Brown scones are full of roughage and great for breakfast. And here is a good tip: you can make this mixture, shape the scones and freeze them. You can then cook the scones straight from the freezer to the oven – just give them an extra 5 minutes and make sure the scones are golden brown and well risen.

Preheat the oven to 220°C (425°F/gas mark 7). Line 2 baking sheets with parchment paper and grease the paper with a little oil.

Sift the flours, baking soda and salt into a bowl. Tip in the bran left in the sieve and stir it in with the wheat bran. Rub in the butter with your fingertips until it is evenly dispersed. Stir in the sugar.

Make a well in the centre of the dry ingredients and add the buttermilk and golden syrup. Using a large spoon, mix gently and quickly until you have achieved a smooth, not-too-sticky dough. Add a little more buttermilk if necessary, until the dough binds together without being sloppy.

On a lightly floured surface, roll out the dough to a 2.5cm (1in) thickness and cut into rounds with a 6cm (2½in) plain cutter. Arrange on the lined baking sheets and bake for 10–15 minutes, until golden brown and well risen. Serve with butter or lightly whipped cream and strawberry jam.

BOXTY

MAKES 4

Boxty is a traditional Irish potato pancake that is different to the more well-known potato farl. They are mostly associated with the north Midlands, north Connacht and southern Ulster, in particular the counties of Mayo, Sligo, Donegal (where it is known locally as poundy or poundies; also known as potato bread in Ulster), Fermanagh, Longford, Leitrim and of course Cavan. There are many variations of the recipe but all contain finely grated raw potatoes and all are served fried. We always serve them in the restaurant as part of our full Irish breakfast, made by Amelda's uncle, Gerry Baxter.

225g (8oz) raw floury potatoes, peeled

225g (8oz) leftover mashed potatoes

50g (2oz) plain flour, plus a little extra for dusting

good pinch of salt

a knob of butter, for frying

Coarsely grate the raw potatoes into a clean tea towel, then wring out all of the excess starchy liquid over a bowl (don't discard it). Tip the squeezed potatoes into a separate bowl and cover with the mashed potatoes.

Once the squeezed-out liquid has settled, the starch drops to the bottom. Carefully pour off the clear liquid from the top and discard, then mix the starch thoroughly with the grated and mashed potatoes. Sift over the flour and a good pinch of salt and knead lightly in the bowl until the dough comes together.

Turn the dough out onto a floured board and roll out into a circle that is about 2cm (¾in) thick, then cut into 4 farls (triangles). Heat a griddle pan or large frying pan over a medium-high heat and add a knob of butter. Add the boxy farls and cook for 6–8 minutes on each side, until golden brown and cooked through. Arrange on a warmed plate and serve at once.

CHAPATTIS

MAKES 4

225g (8oz) plain flour, plus extra for dusting

1 tsp baking powder

1 tsp salt

40g (1½oz) butter, diced and chilled

vegetable oil or clarified butter, to cook

Chapattis are Indian flatbreads that are traditionally served with a stew or curry. To serve, spoon some of the curry down the centre of each chapatti, roll up and serve hot. Once you get the hang of them they are extremely easy to prepare and you'll be making them all the time to accompany your curries.

Sift the flour, baking powder and salt into a bowl. Add the butter and rub it in with your fingertips until the mixture looks like fine breadcrumbs. Make a well in the centre and stir in 6 tablespoons of water to make a stiff but soft dough.

Turn out the dough onto a lightly floured surface and knead gently until smooth, then form into 4 balls, flatten slightly and roll out into 23cm (9in) rounds about 5mm (¼in) thick. Brush with oil or clarified butter, fold them in half, then into quarters, shape back into balls and roll out again.

Heat a heavy-based frying pan or flat griddle over a medium heat. Brush each chapatti in turn with a little more oil or clarified butter. Add a chapatti to the pan and cook for 3–4 minutes, turning frequently and brushing with oil or ghee each time you do.

Remove the chapattis from the pan, then wrap in a clean tea towel and keep warm while you cook the rest. Arrange on a warmed plate and serve at once.

GREEN CHILLI AND CORIANDER FLATBREADS

MAKES 4

4 tbsp thick Greek yoghurt

1 egg, lightly beaten

225g (8oz) self-raising flour,
plus extra for dusting

½ tsp salt

1 green chilli, seeded and
finely chopped

2 tbsp chopped fresh coriander,
plus extra to garnish

sunflower oil, for cooking

about 25g (1oz) butter

These flatbreads are very similar to traditional naan bread, but as they have no yeast in them they are much quicker to make. They are delicious with all kinds of curries but could also be served on the side of a chunky soup. Feel free to play around with the flavourings to suit your own tastes.

Mix the yoghurt with enough warm water to make 120ml (4fl oz) of liquid, then stir in the beaten egg. Sift the flour and salt into a bowl. Make a well in the centre and add the yoghurt mixture along with the chilli and coriander. Quickly mix to a soft but not sticky dough, adding a little extra warm water if necessary.

Turn the dough out onto a lightly floured work surface and knead gently for about 30 seconds, until smooth. Divide into 4 portions, then using a rolling pin, roll out each piece to an oval shape that is no more than 3mm (⅛in) thick.

Heat a large non-stick flat griddle or frying pan over a medium heat. Add a thin film of oil to the heated pan and cook one of the pieces of dough for 4–5 minutes on each side, until cooked through and lightly golden. Remove from the pan, pat dry with kitchen paper, then wrap in a clean tea towel until ready to use. Repeat until you have 4 flatbreads. Spread the warm flatbreads with the butter, garnish with fresh coriander and serve at once.

INDEX